Hooky and the Crock of Gold

When Bunny, disguised as Major Beresford, failed to 'con' a middle-aged lady out of £500, his partner and bedmate became extremely discontented. Dolly was after bigger game anyway – in her view Bunny 'didn't do anything enough, didn't drink enough, make love wildly enough, think big enough . . .'

She set out to enrich and enliven their partnership with a far more ambitious plan; she was to deploy her female wiles to persuade an eccentric young peer, who had recently inherited over a million pounds, to cough up £20,000 of investment in a non-existent company – the proceeds to go to Dolly and Bunny.

To this end the couple have to separate, Dolly to act as the spearhead in her task of charming the rich young mug. But the very separation has unforeseen consequences: new relationships develop, and it is soon apparent that the master plan is doomed to go hopelessly awry.

Laurence Meynell's neat and humorous plotting of novels of suspense is at its strongest here. And there is the splendid dialogue and bar-room banter at which this author excels, not least when Hooky Hefferman is present. The result, connived at by Hooky, is a most confusing and enjoyable shambles, with excitement, humour and – against the odds – a happy ending.

By the same author

A VIEW FROM THE TERRACE (Hale)
THE FORTUNATE MISS EAST (Hale)
THE MAUVE FRONT DOOR (Collins)
THE DEATH OF A PHILANDERER (Collins)
OF MALICIOUS INTENT (Collins)
THE CURIOUS CRIME OF MISS JULIA BLOSSOM (Macmillan)
DEATH BY ARRANGEMENT (Macmillan)
A LITTLE MATTER OF ARSON (Macmillan)
THE FATAL FLAW (Macmillan)
THE THIRTEEN TRUMPETERS (Macmillan)
THE FAIRLY INNOCENT LITTLE MAN (Macmillan)
DON'T STOP FOR HOOKY HEFFERMAN (Macmillan)

HOOKY AND THE CROCK OF GOLD

LAURENCE MEYNELL

M

SBN 333 18765 2

First published 1975 by
MACMILLAN LONDON LIMITED
Associated companies in New York
Dublin Melbourne Johannesburg and Delhi

Printed in Great Britain by
NORTHUMBERLAND PRESS LIMITED
Gateshead

CHAPTER ONE

Murderous ideas can start in the most unexpected places.

At about half-past three on a sunny afternoon in the year 1975 Mrs Phillips, a widow of sixty, was busy in the front garden of Orchard Cottage, a small, comfortable, neo-Georgian house which stands about a mile outside the compact little town of Dalesford in Surrey.

Stella Phillips was dead-heading the huge, luxuriantly grown Albertine rose which was one of the chief glories in a garden well known locally for its beauties.

The new secateurs were justifying the really rather frightening price she had had to pay for them at the Chelsea Flower Show last year; the afternoon was pleasantly warm without being hot; her beloved Albertine was looking magnificent and all the better for the careful attention she was giving it. Stella Phillips was therefore happily and busily engaged and was indeed humming to herself when she was interrupted by the *click* of the latch on the front gate.

She turned in mild surprise to see who it might be. She was not expecting anybody, and such tradespeople who still called – the post, the milk, the laundry – never came in mid-afternoon. On the other hand there were half a dozen possibilities – the Dalesford W.I.; the local Horticultural Society; the Red Cross, in all of which she was interested. The person who had now opened the gate and who was standing, half-apologetically, just inside the front garden obviously, however, had no connection with any of these local concerns.

Mrs Phillips had never seen him before and she looked at him with frank interest. She saw a well set-up figure, wearing an expensive-looking tweed jacket (just for a fleeting second it occurred to her that the jacket was almost aggressively new) and, below green corduroy trousers, a pair of highly polished shoes. The man was a stranger, and Mrs Phillips knew nothing whatsoever about him.

On the other hand the stranger knew a good deal about Stella Phillips. He had, as the saying goes, done his homework. He knew, for instance, that she was a widow; that she had been left if not rich at least comfortably off when her husband died; that she lived alone in Orchard Cottage; and that she was a talented and keen gardener.

'I am so sorry to trouble you,' he began; and Stella Phillips, who was very apt to judge people by their voices, was delighted by his cultured tones; in an age when yowls and howls seemed to be the order of the day it was reassuring to hear English so agreeably spoken. 'I wonder if I might trouble you for a glass of water,' the well-spoken stranger went on. 'My sister, in the car,' he pointed vaguely towards the road, 'has had – well, I'm afraid it's almost a slight heart-attack.'

Stella Phillips's Red Cross proclivities were at once alerted; she was all solicitude.

'Good gracious me,' she said in her friendly way. 'Is she bad? You must bring her in.'

'No, no. I don't want to put you to all that trouble. And she isn't really ill; I mean, it isn't anything immediately dangerous. She's had these turns before, and if I could just have a glass of water—'

'Yes, of course.'

Mrs Phillips peeled off her gloves, put them and the secateurs in the trug among the dead heads of the Albertine, and hurried into the house.

When she came out again in a few moments carrying a glass of water the stranger was profuse in his thanks.

'This really is extremely kind of you.'

'Indeed, it's nothing. Would you like me to come with you to the car?'

'No, please don't bother.'

'If your sister is ill I might be able to do something.'

'It's more than good of you to offer. Let's see what this glass of water does. I think it will buck her up sufficiently to get her home, and that's all that matters at the moment.'

Stella would have liked to accompany him to the car out of mere curiosity, but she had a feeling that to do so might be something of an intrusion and so somewhat reluctantly she waited by the front gate for his return. In a few minutes he was back, empty glass in hand. Stella looked her query at him, and he nodded reassuringly in reply.

'Much better,' he said. 'She's got over this little sharp attack, whatever it was, and now the thing to do is to get her home. She asked me to say that she is extremely grateful to you—'

'Good gracious – a glass of water – I don't feel that I have done anything.'

'On the contrary, you've been a good Samaritan. I'm afraid I haven't introduced myself yet. Major Beresford.'

'And I'm Mrs Phillips.'

The business of formal introduction produced a thoroughly English moment of slight restraint, then Major Beresford said, 'Well, we are both very grateful to you, Mrs Phillips. There is just one other thing if it wouldn't be too much trouble—'

'Of course not. Anything I can do.'

'Would it be possible for me to make a telephone call to arrange for the doctor to be at the house when we get back?'

'Of course; please. Come along in.'

Stella led the way into the house and opened the door of the drawing-room.

'The telephone is on my desk in the window,' she said. 'I'm afraid the desk is a bit untidy. I always seem to have half a dozen letters which need answering somehow. I expect you know the number. Anyway, there's a local directory on the stool at the side. You just dial and get through.'

She pulled the drawing-room door to, and after a moment's hesitation in the hall went out into the front garden again. The drawing-room window was open so that it was possible, without consciously making an effort, to hear most of what Major Beresford was saying; she didn't realise it at the time, of course, but in point of fact he was deliberately speaking loudly enough to make sure that she would hear him.

'... Is that you Miss Dale? Major Beresford here. I'm afraid Lady Lucilla has had another of her attacks.... No.... No. and I've been lucky enough to find someone who has been extremely kind ... and helpful.... Yes.... No, no danger – at least I don't think so; but, all the same, I want you to ring up the doctor to tell him what has happened and ask him to call round to see Lady Lucilla as soon as possible. Would you do that, please?'

Major Beresford replaced the receiver. He had not in fact been speaking to anyone; but that detail was not, of course, known to Mrs Phillips, who was basking in the comforting glow of the Major's references to herself. He came out through the front door and once again Mrs Phillips's ears were charmed by his agreeable, well-bred tones.

'Thank you so much, Mrs Phillips. I got through without any trouble. I'm not sure what the cost of a call is but I have left enough on your desk to cover it, I hope.'

'Really, you shouldn't have bothered,' Mrs Phillips protested.

Major Beresford cut her short with a smile and a raised hand. 'Please,' he said. 'You have been more than kind, and I should hate to abuse your hospitality. What a magnificent rose you have there!'

Mrs Phillips's heart warmed to him still further.

'Oh, are you a gardener?' she asked.

'Only in a very amateurish way, I'm afraid; but I know a beautiful thing when I see it, and you've certainly got one there.'

'Yes. My Albertine. Isn't she lovely? It's not really an ideal position for her, yet somehow she seems to like it there and does splendidly. Of course, she has the drawback of flowering only once, but when she does flower she's superb; and you can't have everything, can you?'

Major Beresford smiled in philosophical agreement. 'Indeed,

you can't,' he said. 'Not with the world in the state it's in today.'

Mrs Phillips nodded energetically. 'Awful, isn't it? Everything so difficult and expensive. Sometimes I really wonder how we shall all go on.'

'I expect you will go on being kind and helpful to people as you have been to my sister and myself this afternoon,' the Major said gallantly, and Mrs Phillips blushed with pleasure.

When the front gate had clicked behind the finally departed Major, Mrs Phillips addressed herself once more to her dead-heading operations; the unexpected and unusual incidents of the afternoon gave her a pleasantly warm glow as she reflected on them.... Lady Lucilla.... She hoped nobody would accuse her of being a snob, but all the same there was something undeniably nice about a title.... Major Beresford. ... What regiment? she wondered.... You couldn't get away from it: Army men, Regular Army men, were always so well bred and polite....

Heartened by these agreeable thoughts she worked away with a will in the warm sunshine of afternoon.

Meanwhile in a Rover saloon parked some fifty yards down the road the well bred and polite Major was reporting to the occupant of the passenger seat. This was a woman in her mid-thirties, a shade too thin, so that her enemies (and she was not without them) would be justified in calling her angular or peaky, but still undeniably good-looking in a hard sort of way.

Her name was not Lucilla and she had no right to any title. Naturally enough she was not suffering from any sort of heart attack, but she was suffering from something which overtook her fairly frequently – a fit of bad temper. She admitted the skill of the con man she worked and lived with but she was growing increasingly tired of him. The theatrical side of him so enjoyed the artistic details of plucking the victim that in her opinion he was apt not to bother enough about the size of the booty. If the woman sitting in the passenger seat, gloomily reflecting on the fact that her thirty-fifth birthday was close at hand and not in the least relishing the prospect, was to continue the partnership, she wanted something better than the small-time *coups* they had been contented with so far.

'Well?' she asked.

'Went like a dream. The old bird was in the front garden doing something to a rose – pruning it, I suppose; and she swallowed everything hook, line and sinker. It's all set for tomorrow now.'

'And how much will she be good for?'

'I shall have to judge that tomorrow. See how she reacts. Feel my way a bit. There's artistry in these things, you know, Dolly.'

'I don't want artistry, I want cash. You're not in the O.U.D.S. now, Bunny. How much are you going to get out of her?'

'I shall try for five hundred, I think. If you open your mouth too wide you scare them off.'

'Five hundred isn't much use,' the woman said sulkily, 'not with what we owe.'

'It's much better than nothing.'

'If we get it!'

At eleven-thirty next morning Stella Phillips, on her way through the hall with a vase of flowers, was surprised to hear the front-door bell ring. She glanced at the long clock standing in the corner. Her brother Andrew was coming to lunch but he surely wouldn't arrive until twelve or after. The morose but invaluable Mrs Mason was busy in the kitchen preparing the meal, so after a second's hesitation Stella put the vase of flowers down on the hall table and went to open the door herself.

She was surprised and, as she had to admit to herself, pleased to see Major Beresford there. Major Beresford as tweedily smart and as agreeably spoken as ever.

Being the kindly person that she essentially was, Stella instinctively greeted him with the query, 'How is Lady Lucilla today? I do hope she is better.' The words were scarcely out of her mouth before she was bitterly regretting them. *Lady Lucilla*; Major Beresford had said nothing to her about Lady Lucilla; he would now know that she had overheard his telephone conversation and might think that she had deliberately listened in to it. She stood self-accused of a social *faux pas* and was dismayed by the thought. Luckily, however, Major Beresford didn't seem to notice anything wrong.

'My sister's still in bed,' he answered, 'but she's a good deal better and she particularly asked me to come and thank you again for all your kindness.' The Major smiled his famous lady-killer smile and added, 'And, of course, I was only too glad of an excuse to do so!'

Really, Stella Phillips thought, what a relief these days to meet such a charmingly polite man. An inspiration suddenly occurred to her; the decanter of sherry and the glasses were already set out against the lunchtime visit of brother Andrew – why shouldn't she offer the well-mannered Major Beresford a glass of sherry? Orchard Cottage didn't entertain much and she was aware that it was rather a daring thing to do, but somehow she felt in the mood to be daring.

'I think it is so nice of you to come back like this just to say "thank you",' she said. 'Please do come in and sit down for a moment and have a glass of sherry.'

The Major's smile increased.

'Well, that's extremely kind of you. A glass of sherry? Yes. Very civilised. I'd like to. But you must excuse me if I stay only a few minutes. I'm on my way to London.'

Inside the drawing-room Major Beresford was very complimentary about everything; the marquetry furniture, the pieces of Chelsea china, the wallpaper all came in for approval. 'Such a relief in these days of poor taste,' he said, 'to find somebody living up to what you and I, dear lady, would call the old standards.'

Nobody minds having their possessions and their good taste praised. Stella Phillips certainly didn't.

'And you yourself live in London?' she asked conversationally.

'No, no. I don't live there. But I'm going up there today. I have to be in the City by three o'clock. It's an important meeting for me. Just one of those lucky opportunities that we all get occasionally, don't we?'

'I suppose we do,' Stella replied vaguely and wishing it were true as far as she was concerned. 'A business opportunity I expect you mean, do you?'

The Major nodded and took a sip of sherry; it struck him as being pretty thin stuff but what he said was, 'I congratulate you on this sherry; it's excellent. Yes, in a way it's business. You and I, dear lady, were both brought up not to talk about money in polite conversation, but these days who can help it? Unfortunately we all just have to think about money a great deal, don't we?'

'I'm afraid I do,' Stella agreed.

'My sister's husband is concerned in property in a big way,' the Major went on. 'I don't pretend to understand all the technical details of the thing. I don't have to; Lucilla's husband is an acknowledged expert in the City, and it is quite sufficient for me to know that he is backing the scheme and giving it his whole-hearted approval. And, of course, going into it himself in a big way. He tells me – and nobody in the City of London knows more about this sort of thing than he does – that City Properties Development Association is going to make a fortune for everybody lucky enough to get into it. Being Lucilla's brother I am being allowed to put in two thousand pounds. In six months' time my shares will be worth five times that amount, ten thousand pounds.'

'Good gracious me,' Stella said, her eyes wide with interest and excitement.

Major Beresford sipped at his thin sherry again and added sagely, 'Of course, that's the thing these days. Property. That's where the money is. It's had its bad patch but it's coming up again. If you're lucky enough to get a foot in that market you can clean up a packet.' He glanced at the French ormolu clock on the mantelshelf and Stella, noting the fact, hoped that he wasn't going to hurry away at once.

'Will you really get ten thousand pounds for the two you are going to put in?' she asked.

'I shall be disappointed if it isn't more.'

'But can anybody buy shares in this development thing you mentioned?'

'City Properties Development Association. No, I'm afraid they can't. Like a lot of these really good things it's pretty much of a closed shop. A family concern. You have to know somebody who knows somebody who's on the inside. You know how it goes.'

'I wish *I* knew somebody,' Stella Phillips said wistfully.

Major Beresford drained his glass of sherry and deliberately took his time over doing so. He appeared to be thinking. In fact he *was* thinking. He was thinking: Thank God for the in-built greed in human nature. What would honest con men do without it? What he said, speaking with apparent reluctance, was, 'I don't say that it's altogether *impossible* in the circumstances. After all, both Lucilla and I both feel very much indebted to you for your kindness yesterday and I'm a great believer in one good turn deserving another. Always have been.' He switched on his friendly, confidence-inspiring smile at its full power for Stella's benefit. 'I believe if I explained what has happened and asked for an extra five hundred shares for a special friend of mine I could get them.'

'Do you really think so, Major?'

'If we don't ask for more than five hundred, yes. I think I might manage that.'

'That would be five hundred pounds?'

'That's it. A pound a share.'

'And you think that in six months' time they will be worth – what did you say? Five times? That's two thousand five hundred, isn't it?'

'At least that. It might well be more.'

'Can you really get them for me?'

'I'll certainly try, Mrs Phillips. There's nobody I would sooner do it for.'

Stella blushed with pleasure. 'And then I'll give you a cheque for five hundred pounds as soon as you tell me,' she said. 'Is that right?'

For answer Major Beresford drew an expensive-looking wallet out of his pocket and from it produced a cheque which he briefly exhibited to Mrs Phillips.

'It's a question of getting in *now*,' he said. 'On the ground floor. Here's my own cheque already made out. The deadline is five o'clock this afternoon. That's why I'm going up to London. After five no application from anybody will be considered. The opportunity ends then.'

'Can't I get in then after all? Couldn't I give you a cheque now to take up for me?'

Major Beresford appeared to be turning this suggestion over in his mind. After a few moments he said, 'Well, yes, I suppose you could, if you really want to.'

'But of course I want to. It's just the sort of lucky chance I never thought I should get. I want to make two thousand pounds profit just as much as anybody else.'

'Of course you do, Mrs Phillips.' The Major was smiling at her again now. 'All right. Give me your cheque and I promise you I'll do my best for you. Where's your bank by the way?'

'I bank locally; here, in Dalesford; Barclays.'

'I see. Good.'

Stella was already crossing to her desk.

'Whom do I make the cheque payable to?' she asked. 'City Property something was it?'

'City Properties Development Association,' Major Beresford said, rolling out the title (of which he was rather proud) with panache, 'but I think you had better make the cheque out to "cash",' he continued. 'As this is strictly speaking a family concern I shall have to do a bit of wangling on your behalf. If I've got the actual money in my hand I think I shall be able to work things.'

'Just as you say,' Stella said, picking up her pen.

As Major Beresford carefully folded and pocketed the cheque he lied magnificently, 'Now all this has got to be strictly business-like,' he announced. 'I shall give you a receipt for this, of course, and then in a day or two I'll call again, if I may, and let you have the actual certificates for your shares.'

'I can't tell you how grateful I am,' was Stella's valedictory blessing.

Brother Andrew, a dry stick, arrived earlier than he had been expected, not many minutes, in fact, after the Major had left. Stella was too full of excitement to keep quiet. She blurted out everything from the moment yesterday when she had been interrupted in dead-heading the Albertine to the Major's polite and generous visit just concluded.

Brother Andrew listened in growing and horrified incredulity; long experience had made him realise that women were fools, but he had still fondly imagined his own sister to have more sense than this.

'Good God,' he interrupted angrily as Stella's bright chatter drew to its close. 'You don't mean to tell me that you have given this man a cheque for five hundred pounds made payable to cash?'

'That's what Major Beresford told me I had to do.'

'Surely to high heaven you must realise that this precious Major Beresford of yours is a first-class swindler?'

'A swindler? I can't believe it.'

'God give me strength. Where do you bank? Barclays, isn't it? I'll ring them up and stop the cheque.'

'Do you really think there's something wrong about his story of the shares and so on?'

Andrew was already on his way to the telephone; he turned round long enough to say, 'I don't think there is anything wrong with it from his point of view. From his point of view it's a clever swindle skilfully carried out. There are lots of people like Major Beresford in the world; all they need in order to thrive is a plentiful supply of what are commonly referred to as suckers. Your Major Beresford found one, and I only hope I'm in time to spoil his little game.'

As a base from which to carry out his carefully planned operation Major Beresford had established himself and the woman he worked with in the Saracen's Head, Dalesford's one good hotel. It was here that Dolly was awaiting his return, lying on the bed fully dressed, smoking and reading the *Daily Express*. She had already packed their two suitcases, since it was standard practice to quit any territory just as soon as a *coup* was successfully concluded.

The moment the man came into the room she could tell that something had gone wrong. She threw the *Express* away and sat up.

'What's happened?'

'I'm not sure really. I don't see where it went wrong.'

'Haven't you got the money?'

'The old dame gave me the cheque all right. No trouble at all. Five hundred quid. She would probably have made it a thousand if I had asked, and I went straight to the bank with it. Damn it, I was at the counter actually cashing the thing when somebody came from behind and said something to the girl and would I step into the manager's office for a moment and have a word about Mrs Phillips's cheque as a message had come through to stop it.'

'And did you?'

'Christ, be your age, Dolly. Of course I didn't. If a message has come through to stop the cheque it means the old lady has got suspicious. God knows why. I sold the thing to her right enough. I'll swear she believed every word of it. But something evidently turned up to make her change her mind; hence the message to the bank.'

'What actually happened at the bank, then?'

'I put on an act, of course.... Couldn't think what they were talking about.... Must be some mistake.... I didn't imagine an old client like Mrs Phillips would enjoy having one of her cheques refused and I was going straight back to Orchard Cottage to find out what was the matter and so on.

So now we've got to get moving as quick as we can.'

'Without any money?'

'Quite right. Without any money. You needn't rub it in.'

The woman ground her cigarette out in the ashtray on the bedside table and said angrily, 'I knew this thing wasn't going to be any good from the word go. Somehow I just knew it. If we go on piddling about with miserable little five-hundred-pound jobs we shan't get anywhere; except in jail,' she added bitterly. 'And now I suppose you haven't got enough to pay the hotel bill, have you?'

'You get the cases out to the car and I'll deal with the office,' the man told her.

They drove back to London in almost total silence. For all the bluff self-assurance which he displayed when acting one of his confidence-trick parts the man whom all his associates knew as Bunny was essentially a weak character, a good deal weaker than the woman he was teamed up with. He was in fact considerably dependent upon her and at times afraid of her. His moods were largely dictated by hers. If Dolly was in good spirits he found it easy to be at his ebullient best; when she was in one of her bad moods he was downcast and nervy. Sexually she had the same sort of dominance over him; he needed her much more than she did him; she let him enjoy her favours only when it pleased her to do so and he sometimes thought she withheld them just for the fun of seeing him frustrated.

Their London flat consisted of no more than two rooms and a cooking-cupboard in a noisy mews close to Marble Arch.

They were both essentially metropolitan people, city animals, who always felt better for returning to the din and jostle and tawdriness of what within living memory used to be the best city in the world to live in. But on this particular day the failure at Dalesford had plunged Dolly into a foul temper. It was temper which arose partly from fear. She was beginning to be scared. She was thirty-five and she desperately wanted money and some sort of security in life; there were moments when she regretted ever having started on a way of living which at the time had seemed to have some glamour and excitement about it.

At the entrance to the mews she had bought an *Evening Standard* and she sat on a low stool in front of the electric fire scanning the headlines with uninterested and cynical eyes. 'What a lot of cock these politicians talk,' she exclaimed. 'Mix me a drink, will you? And make it a good one. After that shambles at Dalesford I want something.'

She watched the man Bunny as he busied himself at the corner cupboard where the bottles were kept. He poured out a large Scotch for her and only a moderate one for himself. That was one thing about him, she thought; he wasn't a lush, as a rule he didn't drink much. She wished suddenly that he *would* drink a lot. That was the fault with him, she realised: he didn't do anything enough; he didn't drink enough, make love wildly enough, think big enough.

When he brought the glass to her she said, 'You've put too much soda in it.'

'I only put a splash.'

'Christ, you've drowned it.'

Bunny held his peace. He saw a row looming up and, although he could be savage-tempered at times, on the whole he disliked rows.

The woman took a generous gulp of the whisky which she alleged to have been drowned and returned to the attack.

'So all that was a pretty good bloody failure, wasn't it?'

'Yes, I'm afraid it was. Better luck next time.'

'That's what you always say. That's the battle cry of the ineffectual. Better luck next time.'

'We haven't done so badly up to date, Dolly.'

'We haven't done so well either, have we? That's the point. I don't want to do not so badly; I want to do well, really well. God, look at the money there is about everywhere, and how much of it are we getting? Even if your wonderful little scheme at Dalesford had come off, what were we going to get out of it? Five hundred. And how long would that have lasted us? We must owe most of that already. It's what I said a moment ago, Bunny; you're ineffectual. In every sort of way.'

The man flushed but kept his temper. 'You don't suppose I enjoyed it going wrong any more than you, do you? It was just one of those things.'

'Just one of those things!'

Bunny, stung by the scorn in her voice, said sharply, 'And, anyway, if you are so god-damned superior about what I do for you, why don't you see if you can do any better yourself?'

The woman had been on the point of throwing the *Standard* to one side, but at the last second a small paragraph at the bottom of the front page caught her eye and she drew the paper to her again.

When she had read the eight-line item she laid the *Standard* down and said quietly, 'You never know. I might do that very thing!'

It had been a name at the end of the news item which had caught Dolly's eye and stirred her memory – Charles Manderville Fenton. The paragraph which included it ran as follows:

PEER COLLAPSES IN WEST END CLUB

A tragedy occurred in the hall of Farnel's, one of London's most exclusive social clubs, this afternoon. Lord Pentallan had just told the hall porter to order a taxi when he collapsed and, in spite of first-aid attention, including an attempt to give the kiss of life, died almost immediately. An inquest will be held tomorrow. The hall porter Arthur Stamp (62) said, 'It's not the sort of thing we like to happen in the Club.' Lord Pentallan was in his seventieth year and was unmarried. It is understood that the title and a fortune estimated at one and a quarter million pounds including a country property near Farnbridge in the Hertfordshire commuter belt will pass to a nephew, Mr Charles

Manderville Fenton, at present holding an executive post in the City.

Twelve years ago it had been; and now it all came back to her vividly. Twelve years ago she had been twenty-three and in many ways a lot, lot younger than she had now become. There had been no Bunny then, no confidence tricks. She had been on the fringe of the entertainment world then, knocking hard to gain entrance and never quite succeeding. There had been some bits and pieces in a repertory company, one leading part with good notices which for a moment looked like her breakthrough and two appearances on the box. In the end it didn't come to anything; it petered out into the heartbreaking routine: Shaftesbury Avenue in the rain; trudging up the narrow stairs to the agent's office on the third floor; the perpetual explanations and excuses: 'Not just at this moment, I'm afraid.... Nobody wants that sort of thing these days.... Maybe when we get all this Christmas nonsense out of the way ... but don't ring us please; if anything does come along we'll ring you....'

They didn't ring, or only very seldom; but at twenty-three your optimism could stand a lot of shocks. At twenty-three, sharing a minute flat with a girl chum; gay, good-looking, good fun; always ready to join any party, rout, fiesta or celebration from a bring-your-own-bottle shambles in a Bloomsbury basement to the occasional long dress and all you've got in the way of jewellery at the Berkeley. At twenty-three you managed somehow to have a pretty good time without ever being quite sure where the next week's share of the rent was coming from.

Mavis Toller paid the other half of the rent. Mavis, a little older, and in those days a little harder and a little more experienced. Mavis, since lost sight of in the chopping and changing maelstrom of life, but in that flat-sharing time a good off-sider, a great buddy; always ready for a laugh; always quick with cynical advice about how to cope with men and keep them in their place (this usually accompanied by a hilariously bawdy comment).

The two of them had been together, twelve years ago, at Maidenhead. For the life of her the woman couldn't now remember how it was that they were in that spuriously luxurious and ruinously expensive place on the river; but there they were, and suddenly she could vividly recall the dim lighting, the noise, the lushy-plushy feeling of a crowded room, a jukebox playing and two white-coated barmen with busy, expert hands and cold, tired eyes.

Suddenly the bar was invaded by the other party, an insurging of half a dozen rowdy, cheerful young males completely confident that the world belonged to them and that everything was theirs for the taking.

Mavis surveyed them with cynical amusement. Young and foolish and drink-filled as they were, there might be pickings, she thought.

It turned out that there was to be a wedding next day ('good old Jonah' was getting spliced) and this was the traditional stag party of the evening before.

Stag party it might be; but two good-looking girls sitting on high stools at the bar and showing a tantalising amount of silk-clad leg were hardly likely in the circumstances to go unnoticed.

Before long Dolly and Mavis were in the thick of things, being included in every round of drinks and roaring with laughter, as everybody else did, at the unceasing stream of jokes about good old Jonah and what his whale would do to him on the bridal night.

One of Jonah's friends, by looks the youngest and most innocent, attached himself particularly to Dolly. He was eighteen and had just entered Worcester College, Oxford. The good-looking girl of twenty-three, sitting up on her high stool at the bar seemed like a sophisticated woman of the world to him.

Young Charles Manderville Fenton thought he was seeing life. There was a lot of drinking and a lot of talking. In the way of young men who are not strictly sober Charles Fenton told Dolly a great deal about himself and what he proposed to do in the world; about art, politics and religion; about what was wrong with everything and how it ought to be put right; about how smashing she looked and how lonely life was sometimes when you were just starting at Oxford.

It was all pretty juvenile stuff, which was not in the least surprising because at eighteen Charles Manderville Fenton was still a pretty juvenile person; it is doubtful if he even entertained any serious thoughts of a conquest of Dolly. If he did, they never materialised. She did accompany him for a walk along the river bank 'to get some fresh air for a moment'; there was a bit of inexpert fumbling and an unsatisfactory kiss; but that was as far as things went and as far as Dolly wanted them to go; she thought Charles Manderville Fenton was a young ass without any money.

Now, of course, he wouldn't be so young, but he might still be an ass and it seemed that he was going to have a lot of money.

The woman of thirty-five who had come a long way in the last twelve years finally threw the *Evening Standard* to one side. She repeated what she had already said to the unambitious man of whom she was growing tired. 'You never know. I might do that very thing!'

CHAPTER TWO

Hooky Hefferman had no official connection with the newspaper world these days. Nevertheless, he frequently found himself wandering along Fleet Street for old times' sake; and, as he was in the habit of pointing out, no sane man would pass El Vino without looking in, if only to get the flavour of things, to be amused by the gossip and rumours, the speculations and reminiscences, the low-down and the lies of the best sounding-board in London. As Hooky himself had once said, 'In the papers you get what the different editors want you to think is the news; in El Vino you get the news.'

On this particular morning the place was unusually quiet when he turned in from the Street, but he was pleased to see at least one familiar figure propping up the bar in the accustomed spot.

Boozey French wrote a scabrous social column for a scabrous paper owned by somebody whom he himself frequently referred to as a scabrous Lord: 'Things I Hear about Town'. 'Human nature being what it is, you get 'em both ways', as Boozey was wont to point out. 'Half of the silly buggers are terrified they're going to be left out and they won't see their stupid names in print, and the other half are scared to death of finding themselves in. So they all read it.'

Nobody was certain of Boozey's age. Fifty-five? people guessed. Sixty? Sixty-five even. Age, dissolution, decay and death were taboo subjects with Boozey. Maybe because they came too near home. As far as anyone knew, he existed on an exclusive diet of tobacco and alcohol. Nobody was certain where he lived, or when – if ever – he slept. He was possessed of two eyes, two arms, two legs and, presumably, the usual equipment of a male human being but, although he was capable of biting witticisms about women, he had never been known to be intimate with one. He had an apparently inexhaustible fund of hilariously funny dirty stories, but these he had recently ceased to retail. 'I never believe in being second-best,' he explained, 'and these days no one can compete in the c—— and f—— business with the Royal Court Theatre or the West End cinemas. I know when I'm beaten.'

Boozey was a lonely, ill, embittered man; and a perpetually thirsty one.

'Just in time,' he greeted Hooky, draining his glass and pushing it across the counter. 'I'll have an exceedingly large Scotch.'

Hooky didn't mind subsidising Boozey French; in a way he could almost like the man; he ordered a Pimms No. 1 for himself and asked, 'What news on the Rialto, Boozey?'

'None, thank God,' Boozey answered. 'Or none that I know of, anyway. News is a damned nuisance; it gets in the way of my column; if there's any news, or what he imagines is news, floating around, the Lord is apt to get on to the telephone (that man practically lives on the blasted instrument) to tell me to chase off after it. Me, go chasing things! Christ, I've got more sense. My chasing days are over. It's a great mistake to chase anything – dollars, dollies or dreams. I wouldn't chase the Golden Fleece itself if I saw it at the end of the street.'

'I don't think you're likely to do that, Boozey.'

'Not now, chum; no, not now. I did once. Caught a glimpse of it anyway. Or thought I did. The blasted thing vanished into thin air. Life's great disappearing trick that sucks us all in. I don't want news now. Give me a bottle of Bell's and two hours alone with my typewriter and I'll turn out exactly the sort of column the Lord wants without any interference from reality. Reality is the great illusion.'

'That's quite an apophthegm, Boozey.'

'I'm astonished you know the word; and even in the Welfare madhouse state you can't expect to get apophthegms for nothing, can you? They have to be paid for.' He pushed his glass forward again, and Hooky nodded to the barman.

Whilst the drinks were being attended to, a younger man breezed in from the street, a camera slung over one shoulder. Boozey regarded him sourly. 'Ask him, if you're after news,' he advised Hooky. 'One of Tom Dorsett's crew on the *Peephole.* Not yet dry behind his ears; but knows it all, of course.'

The young man with the camera obviously didn't know everything, however, because he was very soon enquiring where Lushington Gardens was.

Boozey, for a man who boasted that he never went anywhere, had an astonishing knowledge of London; his way about it was charted by the names of pubs and he instantly supplied the information.

'Chelsea. Go down that dreary King's Road till you come to the Marquis of Hereford. Turn left there and you're in Lushington Gardens. Don't go into the Hereford. The barmaid there will eat you alive. She likes 'em young and inexperienced – two conditions which she is apt to alter with astonishing rapidity. She ought to have a warning label round her neck: *Seduction whilst you wait. Young men led astray at shortest notice.* What's happening in Lushington Gardens?'

'The paper wants a pic of this chap who has come into one and a quarter million. Apparently his father had heart failure and handed in his chips in Farnel's in St James's yesterday. Did you see the para in last night's *Standard* and the marvellous quote from the hall porter: "It's not the sort of thing we like to happen in the Club"?'

'See it?' Boozey echoed indignantly. 'I wrote it. I made it up. Hall porters don't talk like that, but people want to believe they do. And it wasn't his father who died yesterday; it was his uncle. Old Pentallan, who has faithfully attended in the Lords ever since he succeeded to the title eighteen years ago and has had the extreme good sense not to open his mouth there once. He has kept his trap shut and picked up his eight quid a day attendance money like a man. Do you realise that the Lords Spiritual and Temporal of this Realm, the ladies and gentlemen who for various reasons have been dished out with titles and shoved upstairs to get them out of the way, number well over a thousand? That's eight thousand quid a day just for being there when they all turn up. If I had a couple more Scotches I could tell you what that comes to in a year. And it's one hell of a lot of money; more than you make, Hefferman!'

'Considerably more,' Hooky agreed.

'How are things? How's business?'

Hooky made a grimace. 'But I'm an optimist,' he said. 'I expect something will turn up.'

'Your toes probably,' Boozey told him.

It was four o'clock before Hooky found himself heading homewards again. The rain and clouds of the morning had gone; London, that old and battered tatterdemalion, managed to look almost attractive in the afternoon sunshine; even the tawdriness of Soho was transmuted by the mellow light into something not entirely unacceptable.

Along Gerrard Street Hooky noted, subconsciously almost, the familiar landmarks. The 'salvation man' standing patiently in the gutter, his sandwich-board boldly announcing 'Jesus Is Coming Tomorrow. Are You Ready?'; then on one corner of Gerrard Mews the large and flourishing porn-shop, on the other the musical store.

It was into Gerrard Mews that Hooky turned; at the end of that short cul-de-sac stood Regency House, on one floor of which Hooky lived, moved and had his being and where he conducted his ailing business. 'H. H. R. Hefferman,' the legend ran, 'Private Investigator. Every sort of Confidential Enquiry undertaken.' He had hardly set foot inside the front door of Regency House before he was pounced upon by an agitated Roly Watkins. Roly Watkins was the caretaker and factotum of the place, long since recognised by Hooky as being indispensable and infuriating in about equal proportions.

That very day, in Hooky's absence, Roly had undergone

a traumatic experience, and the effects of it were still visibly on him.

'Thank Gawd you're back, Mr H.,' was his welcome. 'Where-ever you bin? The North Pole or somewhere? I thought you were never coming. Oh dear, what a calamity.' A succession of possibilities flickered through Hooky's mind: the landlord had come to demand why last quarter's rent was still unpaid; a man from the telephone department with unpleasant talk about 'cutting you off unless'; some charmer for an evening to whom, under the joint and persuasive influences of Venus and Bacchus, too much had been inadvisedly said, or even – Heaven forbid – promised.

Any one of these normal hazards of existence would have been awkward and unwelcome; but they all faded into harmless insignificance when Roly next spoke.

'*She's* been here. The Honourable Mrs Hoity-Toity. That aunt of yours.'

Hooky felt for a chair and sank into it. This was serious indeed.

The Honourable Mrs Theresa Page-Foley was not only his aunt; she was the quintessence of Auntism: upright, unbending; of the old school; brought up in and remembering the old standards; at the age of eighty still demanding just as much from herself as from everybody else.

For some years now this formidable old lady had lived by herself in a flat in Hove, playing bridge with anyone she could dragoon into a game and looking out with grim dismay on a world whose crudities and cheapness she disliked and despised.

Although he found her somewhat terrifying, there were moments when Hooky felt bound to honour family obligations by a duty visit to Hove; but his Honourable Aunt safely tucked away in Hove was one thing, his Honourable Aunt here, on the doorstep in Gerrard Mews, no doubt roaring about like a lioness seeking whom she might devour, was something else again.

'My Gawd, the old lady put me through it,' Roly continued. 'They want to get 'er down to Wellington Barracks; half those man-eating sergeant-majors could go off on leave then; she'd do their job for them all right. Oh dear.'

'And what did my aunt want?' Hooky enquired.

'You.'

Hooky blanched slightly. 'Why?' he asked.

'Ah, she didn't say *why*. She's not one to say *why*, that aunt of yours isn't, Mr H. *Where* is what she was on about. *Where is 'e?* she kept asking me. *Where is 'e?*'

'What did you say, Roly?'

'What would you expect me to say? All women are the same; don't matter whether it's one of the Honourable nobs like your aunt or Mary Ellen from round the corner, they always want to know too much – what a man's doing, where 'e's been, why 'e isn't doing something else or been somewhere different. Us men 'ave got to stick together, Mr H., or by golly they've got us by the what-you-may-call-'ems. I *knew* where you were, of course, give or take a name or two. I knew it was in the saloon bar of the Magpie and out of that into the saloon bar of the Swan and end up in the saloon bar of the Black Boy. But I wasn't going to tell that to your Honourable Aunt, was I? No fear. I daren't for one thing. " 'e's out on a job," I said. "A highly important and confidential mission for a member of 'Er Majesty's Government." '

'Remind me to give you a raise next time I pay you anything,' Hooky said.

'Not that she believed a word of it, Mr H.'

'She didn't?'

'Not a blind dicky bird. "Well," she said, "if the public houses close at half-past three, which I imagine may be the case, I presume Mr Hefferman may be back here round about four. Let him know I shall call again shortly afterwards." So now I'm letting you know, Mr H., as per instructions from 'Is Master's Voice; and, if you'll excuse me, I'm off for a breather. I don't want to be here when the Honourable Day of Judgement calls. I don't feel equal to facing that lot again.'

But when Theresa Page-Foley reappeared in Gerrard Mews

things went much more smoothly than might have been expected. True that her opening gambit had a familiar touch of tartness about it.

Entering Hooky's room, which was on the first floor, she fired her first broadside without preamble.

'That staircase of yours is disgustingly dirty, Hooky, and in parts dangerous.'

'I'm sorry about that, Aunt.'

'That little ferrety-faced man who told me all those lies this morning about where you were—'

'Roly Watkins?'

'I can believe that that is his name. He looks the sort of person who would be called Roly Watkins. I strongly suggest that you equip him with a pail and a scrubbing-brush and some cleaning-rags and set him to work. A few days' hard work would probably do him a lot of good.'

Having relieved her feelings by handing out this typical piece of advice, Mrs Page-Foley astonished Hooky by lapsing into a mood which, for her, bordered on amiability. Hooky – consumed with curiosity on the matter – ventured to ask what had brought her to London.

'Not love of the place,' she told him, 'you may be sure of that. The West End is dirty, untidy and slovenly. Every theatre or cinema one passes has apparently only one subject to talk about – the naked human body. For a very long time now I have been quite well aware what the human body looks like, and generally speaking I consider it a very disappointing spectacle; I'm certainly not going to pay three pounds to sit in the stalls of a West End theatre to stare at it. I came up from Hove for the Annual General Meeting of ROLSA.'

What the hell is ROLSA? Hooky wondered; but he didn't dare to ask; he nodded in what he hoped was a bright, intelligent way.

'Everything go all right with the Rolsians?' he asked.

'Admirably. That old fool Cassonburg was in the chair, and I had the great pleasure of giving him a piece of my mind. I enjoyed doing that, of course; and then to my astonishment a proposal was made that in view of the long time that I have been a member of ROLSA and of what they were kind enough to call my distinguished services to it I should be made an Honorary Life Member.'

'Good for you, Aunt.'

'It's absurd, of course, to let oneself feel pleased by these so-called honours, but the fact is that one *is* pleased by them. There is something else which might have brought me to London; something which, in a way, I ought to do, but I am tired now and I want you to do it for me.'

'Anything I can, of course. Anything at all.'

'Anything to get rid of me, you mean. Quite right too. Young children should be seen and not heard; old bores should be neither heard nor seen. I don't know whether you ever read any newspaper other than the *Sporting Life*. Probably not. But if you do you may have seen a paragraph about Percy Pentallan's death in Farnel's in St James's.'

Hooky nodded. Until he had seen the news item in the *Standard* he had not even been aware that such a person as Lord Pentallan existed, but it did not surprise him in the least that his aunt knew; he had long since realised that if the editors of *Debrett's Peerage* and *Burke's Landed Gentry* both fell down dead simultaneously his Aunt Theresa could without any trouble supply sufficient information from the back of her head to keep the two publications going.

'At one time,' she was now saying, 'I knew Percy Pentallan very well. Very well indeed. I knew his brother George, too. Percy never married; hence there is no direct heir. George did marry and he had a son Charlie. I saw quite a lot of Charlie as a boy. He was an insufferable little ass, and I dare say he is just the same now. But I was friendly with both his father and his uncle, and I think it would be nice if you went round to see him and took my condolences. Your advice is not likely to be of much use to the boy, but if you have nothing better to do – and of course you won't have – you might see if you can give him a helping hand in any way. For one thing I expect he'll be pestered to death by the newspaper people, and at any rate you could fend them off for him.'

How worldly-wise and percipient his indomitable old aunt had been was made evident to Hooky a minute or two after he entered the saloon bar of the Marquis of Hereford. Hooky, an amateur of pubs and keenly responsive to their different tones and ambiences, liked the Hereford immediately.

The Junoesque figure behind the bar with the piled-up golden hair and the alarming cleavage was no doubt the man-eater about whom Boozey French had spoken warningly in El Vino. Running an expertly appraising eye over her, Hooky could well believe that Boozey's words had been justified; he made a mental note there and then that a return visit to the Marquis must figure in his engagement list in the not far distant future. Colourful experience had made Hooky Hefferman only too well aware of the fact that the female of the species was more dangerous than the male; unfortunately for him he liked it that way. The short, dark, foxy-faced customer talking to the man-eater was a stranger to Hooky; yet one single, searching glance told Hooky a lot about him. Everything about the man shrieked *Press*.

'... One and a quarter millions,' Foxy-face was saying. 'That's worth finding in your Christmas stocking; that's better than a poke up the backside from a non-conformist minister; isn't it?'

'Much better,' the man-eater agreed composedly, adding, 'Please don't start using bad language in here. I don't like it. This isn't the BBC.'

Hooky caught Foxy-face's eye and asked, 'Lushington Gardens?'

'Just come from it. You on your way there?'

'I thought of looking in.'

'Press?'

'Sort of.'

'Well, the best of British luck to you, chum. You'll enjoy yourself. Cripes, what a circus! That lunatic will be lucky if he doesn't have his name plastered all over the front page tomorrow. He'd have a job to fight his way out of a paper bag, but at one point he was offering to take on all the Fleet Street boys single-handed. My God, they gave him a ragging. There's one of them still there; still at it; one of Tom Dorsett's lot, trying to get pics and leading this million-and-a-quarter cove one hell of a dance.'

Hooky drained the drink he had ordered and prepared to leave. Dark, slumbrous eyes regarded him steadily.

'Going already?' full red lips enquired.

'Duty calls unfortunately,' Hooky answered, 'but never fear; I'll be back one of these days.'

The man-eater took frank assessment of the burly, broad-shouldered frame and of the chunky, humorous face; then she smiled slowly.

'I hope you will,' she said. 'I should like that.'

The flat in Lushington Gardens was on the first floor; the argument was taking place on the small landing, literally half in and half out of the front door.

As yet undiscovered, Hooky paused halfway up the stairs to get the flavour of things.

The cub reporter from *Peephole* was enjoying himself. Nothing pleases your newspaperman more than the interviewee who loses his temper and inadvisedly says a lot of things which next morning he will bitterly regret but which will make hilarious reading for a few million people.

The *Peephole* man might be only a cub interviewer but he had already learnt most of the dirty tricks of his trade – the prodding, the provoking, the loaded question, the innocent-sounding suggestion. Hooky listened in saddened astonishment to the inept lunacy with which Charles Manderville Fenton (now indeed the new Lord Pentallan) was trying to cope with the situation, blustering in one sentence, almost piteously begging for consideration in the next. He sounded more like a youth of eighteen coming up against a hostile world for the first time than a man of thirty who had just inherited a million plus.

'Can I quote you on that, Lord Pentallan?' *Peephole* was saying.

'Quote what you like. What the devil do the newspapers matter anyway? Written by fools to be read by fools.'

'You don't think much of the man in the street, I take it?'

'I despise the man in the street.'

Hooky groaned; he could see the *Peephole* headlines already: *New Peer* (£1¼ *million*) *says 'I despise man in street'*.

'Now, if I could just get a picture of you in the flat—'

'I don't want you in the flat; I don't want any photographs taken in the flat.'

'Nothing to hide in there, is there, Lord Pentallan?'

'I've told you all I'm going to. Now please leave me, *please*.'

'I expect with this fortune you've come into you'll be thinking of marrying. Can I say there is any romance in the air?'

'I don't want to discuss—'

Hooky moved out of the shadows on the staircase up on to the landing. He laid a hand on the shoulder of the young reporter from *Peephole*; a casual sort of grip; it could have been put there in easy-going greeting, or just possibly there might be a bit of something more forceful behind it.

When he spoke, Hooky's voice matched his grip; it was pleasant enough, but it had an edge on it.

'Buzz off, little love-bird,' he said. 'The interview's over.'

'I just want to get a pic.'

'Lord Pentallan says no pic.'

'I only want a little one.'

'That's what the girl said to the soldier; but it didn't make any difference. No pics. Buzz off.'

The cub reporter knew Hooky well by sight, a frequenter of El Vino; a buddy of the legendary Boozey French, who in turn was quids in with the young man's own irascible boss Tom Dorsett; but he was loath to relinquish his prey.

Hooky's grip tightened ever so slightly, his voice hardened by the same degree.

'Don't push your luck, chum,' he advised. 'Go whilst the going's good.'

The young man hesitated, but he had the sense to recognise that the alarm bells were ringing.

'Well, I've had a bit of fun,' he said defiantly and he went.

Later, in Gerrard Mews, Hooky relaxed. He had undressed and put on a tattered silk dressing-gown, a disreputable garment and one which, had he been married, would instantly have been condemned to the rubbish bin; thus clad and with a large final glass by his side Hooky sank luxuriously into the only comfortable chair in the place and, toasting himself before the electric fire, considered the events of the evening.

He had a good deal to consider.

The two hours that he had spent in the flat in Lushington Gardens had been—he found it was difficult to sum them up; in some ways astonishing, in some ways embarrassing; at times ludicrously trivial, at times rather remarkable.

What the hell could you make of such a potpourri of a human being as young Charles Fenton? he thought, halfway between anger at such contrariness in a man and amusement at it.

As soon as the *Peephole* photographer had left, Hooky had found himself in the flat. Whether he had been invited in or had just gone in he now honestly couldn't remember. Scarcely was he inside than he realised to his acute embarrassment that the new Lord Pentallan was in tears.

'Beastly people; beastly, beastly people,' Charles was saying, 'with their horrible, vulgar newspapers. Why can't they just leave me alone?'

Hooky was not used to men crying and for a moment was at a loss how to deal with the situation.

'What's it got to do with them,' the tearful complaint was continuing, 'how much I inherit, or what I do with it, or – or – or *anything*? They all ought to be locked up and horsewhipped.'

Hooky had never seen a man horsewhipped; in fact, he had

very seldom seen a horsewhip, and he couldn't imagine anybody less likely to use one than the figure now standing opposite him. A figure which suddenly tossed its head, brushed its tears away and said in only too obvious self-satisfaction, 'I didn't give much away though, did I? They didn't get much out of me after all. I think I'm a match for that lot all right.'

Well, if you believe that you'll believe anything, Hooky thought; if you believe that you must be the greatest self-deluder of all time. He spied a row of bottles set out on a side table and it occurred to him that, although he was in somebody else's flat, it was up to him to initiate some sensible action.

He crossed the room and said, 'I think a drink would do us both good, don't you? What's yours?'

'A crême de menthe.'

This made even Hooky hesitate in his tracks for a second. *Chacun à son goût* had long been a cardinal principle in his tolerant life, but even he had to admit that there were times when the *goût* was a shade too outlandish to be accepted easily.

'You drink crême de menthe?' he enquired.

Lord Pentallan nodded briskly.

'Yes, rather, I like it. At the end there; in the odd-shaped bottle; a nice long one, please; I feel I need something after all that stupid business.'

Luckily, next to 'the odd-shaped bottle' there was a bottle of more ordinary, reassuring design, full of good malt whisky. Hooky dealt with the drinks and, handing the green horror to his host, said, 'Well, if that doesn't rot your guts nothing will. Here's fun and, by the way, congratulations on your title.'

It wasn't until that moment that it occurred to Lord Pentallan to enquire who his visitor was and how it had come about that he had appeared so fortunately upon the scene.

'I wondered when you were going to ask about that,' Hooky said. 'I might be another pressman.'

'My God, don't say that!' The new Lord was so upset that for a moment Hooky was afraid he might burst into tears again.

'Take it easy, take it easy. Cast your mind back to your youth. Do you remember a Mrs Page-Foley?'

'Mrs Page-Foley? Heavens, yes, I remember her perfectly well. A frightful old woman. Do you mean to say she's still alive?'

'She's not as frightful as all that, chum; and she's still very much alive, believe you me.'

'I always hated her.'

'She didn't go all that much on you, either.'

'Looking back on things, I'm inclined to think she must have been rolling an eye at my father.'

'Under God all things are possible,' Hooky said piously.

'Of course, my father was a fool.'

In which case he certainly bred true to type, Hooky wanted to say; but he refrained and contented himself with an explanation of his mission as bearer of condolences and good wishes from his aunt.

'Is Mrs Page-Foley your aunt?'

Hooky nodded. 'We all have our crosses in life,' he said.

'Pretty grim, isn't it?'

Hooky often harboured some rather severe thoughts about his Aunt Theresa but, human loyalties being the illogical twisted things they are, he was not prepared to have other people voicing similar views.

'Not as grim as you appear to think, chummo,' he answered. 'The old lady gets a lot of things right. She told me, for instance, that in all probability you would make a balls of being interviewed by the Press. She said the Fleet Street boys would have the pants off you in no time. And, by God, how right she was!'

Mention of the Press had the effect of changing Pentallan's attitude from cocksure arrogance to apprehension.

'Do you suppose they will come round again?' he asked anxiously.

'Does a duck swim?'

'And follow me down to the country, to Pentallan Hall?'

'Like ferrets.'

'It ought not to be allowed in a civilised country.'

'In a civilised country very probably it wouldn't be. We're not living in a civilised country. We're living in a small clearing in the middle of a bloody great jungle.'

'I suppose I ought to hire one of those bodyguards or private detectives or whatever they call them.'

'They're apt to come expensive.'

'What's a few pounds compared to privacy and peace? And, anyway, I haven't got to worry about money now, have I?'

'True, true.'

'How much would I have to pay?'

'Oh, I'd be content with, say, sixty a week plus all expenses.'

Pentallan looked up sharply.

'*You* would?' he asked.

Hooky grinned reassuringly at him. 'Yes, me. The job's just up my street. It's the sort of thing I do and, if you'll forgive a spot of advertising, do rather well; and since my aunt was a great friend of both your late father and uncle it'll be keeping it in the family more or less, won't it? I'll go down with you for a few weeks to shoo the newspaper boys off. If you keep your trap shut and don't do anything silly for a month they'll get tired of you and go chasing off after somebody else.'

CHAPTER THREE

From an aesthetic point of view the best thing about Pentallan Hall is that it is so well screened by some splendid elms and beeches that the house itself is not unduly prominent. It was built in the 1860s, the great period of Victorian vulgarity, and ranks high among the many examples of the domestic-gothic-plus-sham-castle school which is more generally described as the early alcoholic style.

None of which affected Hooky Hefferman in the slightest degree.

Knocked into shape by some pretty sharp buffeting in different parts of the world, Hooky had acquired a certain number of useful attributes, such as knowing when to stand pat and bluff it out on two small pairs; the ability to distinguish blindfold between half a dozen Scotch whiskies; a sense of the infinite wonder of all things created, plus a keen appreciation of the ridiculous nature of most human activities. He could judge a shapely pair of legs as well as any man, but architecture left him cold; what Hooky bothered about was the inside of a house, and he was finding the inside of Pentallan Hall extremely satisfying.

He was enjoying himself.

He was perfectly well aware that in a few weeks' time the *dolce far niente* business would begin to pall; the old urges and itches would come back, the desire to see Boozey French propping up one end of the bar at El Vino and proposing his well-known toast 'to faith, hope, charity and other absent friends'; but for the moment it was pleasant not to be troubled by these idiocies; for the moment he was on holiday, enjoying life from a deck-chair. And incidentally picking up sixty nice clean pound-notes each week and having remarkably few outgoings.

His room in the Hall was known as the Admiral's Room. The name appeared in a narrow passage leading to the butler's pantry where high up on the wall hung a long line of bells each with its appropriate legend: the Drawing Room, the Small Drawing Room, the Study, the Morning Room, the Gun Room, the Blue Room, the Admiral's Room, His Lordship's Room, Her Ladyship's Room, the North-West Room and so on.

Hooky's bedroom was a square lofty place fitted with dark, heavy furniture; to Hooky's great delight its principal feature was a huge four-poster bed, and since one of his minor ambitions in life had always been to sleep in a four-poster he was happy. At half-past seven every morning Skipton brought in an early cup of tea.

Skipton was efficient and reticent in almost equal degrees; you got the impression that Pentallan Hall, the enduring place, mattered a lot more to him than the people who happened to inhabit it at any one time. It was a point of view with which Hooky had a good deal of sympathy. In any case, he admired competence, and Skipton was above all things competent.

Breakfast was at a quarter to nine, and one of the unexpected traits in the generally unpredictable Charles was that he was a stickler for punctuality. Often enough he had been up for some time busying himself nervously with half a dozen begun and soon abandoned activities. Hooky resolutely refused to be concerned with such goings-on; in a life for the most part cheerfully devoid of principles, never to go to bed before midnight and never to do anything active before breakfast had long been one of his few established ones.

Each day after breakfast the *dolce far niente* idea came into full operation, much to Hooky's satisfaction. Professionally he was not without a conscience and he was glad therefore that in the first few days of being at the Hall he had done at least something to justify his presence there. It had not amounted to much simply because not much had needed to be done. The elderly Lord Pentallan who had so thoughtlessly inconvenienced Farnel's by having a fatal heart-attack in the front hall of the Club was never a figure in the public eye; then hard on the heels of his Lordship's death came an even bigger crop than usual of earthquakes, floods, minor wars, major strikes, of bombs being found in basements and of blonde bombshells being found in cabinet ministers' beds so that for the most part the Press lost interest in the Pentallan affair after the small flurry of the first couple of days.

There were two exceptions, the first of which Hooky discovered in the Pentallan Arms making preliminary enquiries before the projected final assault on the Hall itself. She was wearing a black shirt and tight, blue trousers over a behind which God had not intended for trousers; she was disposing of gin and tonics at an alarming rate; she was bright, breezy and hard as nails; she had all the qualities, in fact, which Hooky most actively disliked in women. She was Peggy Shelton of Peggy Shelton's page, a weekly potpourri of astounding inaccuracy and bloody-minded bitchiness, two attributes which made it immensely popular.

Tom Pacey, the landlord of the Pentallan Arms, was a well-mannered man and he was enduring with politeness the barrage of questions to which he was being subjected; but he was not enjoying himself; he was old-fashioned enough to think the world was a more pleasant place when ladies behaved like ladies. He was relieved when Hooky came in. Hooky had discovered the Arms within a few hours of arriving at the Hall. He was a pub man. He had an affinity with pubs. Dumped down on a pitch-black night in an unknown countryside without anyone to give him directions Hooky would have circled round a couple of times like a homing pigeon getting its bearings and then set off straight as an arrow for the nearest local.

He was a great assessor, too, of the character of a pub; and he liked the Arms from the word go: a long low bar; no chromium; no juke-boxes; no canned music; tables scrubbed white; a log fire burning merrily; beer from the wood; Tom

Pacey grave and courteous and full of good stories – it was the sort of inn which almost persuaded you into thinking that perhaps, after all, the good times were not gone forever.

'If it's information about the Hall you're wanting, Miss, this gentleman will be able to tell you,' Tom Pacey said as Hooky came in.

Hooky took in the situation at a glance; in fact, he knew Peggy Shelton by sight and was not entirely surprised to see her there. Where the prey is there also shall the jackals be gathered together. She turned to greet him with hard, bright eyes and a hard, bright smile.

'You're a friend of Lord Pentallan's?' she asked eagerly.

Hooky, who when occasion demanded it was an expert liar, slid into top gear at once.

'I was a friend of his uncle, the old Lord.'

'Really?'

'I knew the old boy well. I was with him when he went down with a heart attack in Farnel's.'

The eyes of the gossip-hungry jackal glistened.

'You weren't, were you?'

'Indeed, I was. I heard the old boy's last words.'

'What did he say?'

'He said, "This will make a nice tit-bit for some of those bloody long-nosed women journalists."'

Tom Pacey moved diplomatically to the far end of the bar where he could laugh unnoticed, and Peggy Shelton refreshed herself with a long swig at the gin and tonic. She took a second look at the tall, square-shouldered man with the chunky face and said, 'I think I'm going off you a bit.'

'For this relief much thanks. Shakespeare somewhere. A great boy for quotes is the Bard; he's always coming in handy.'

'Don't be like that. I just want to do a nice chatty para about young – what's his name? Charlie, isn't it? – about young Charlie Pentallan, whether he's got any special girl-friends and if there is any romance in the air and so on.'

'He's engaged to a black bus-conductress from Smethwick –

if you know where that is; I don't – and Enoch Powell is going to be godfather to their children if they have any.'

'How I wish it were true. Do you suppose I can have an interview with him?'

'Why not?'

Peggy Shelton drained her glass.

'I knew you were going to be helpful as soon as you came in,' she said. 'How far off is this Hall place?'

'Pentallan Hall? What do you want to go there for?'

'You don't look stupid,' Peggy said, 'but I'll try to explain in words of one syllable: I want to have an interview, a cosy little heart-to-hearter, with Charlie boy.'

'Ah, then you'll have to go to the Algarve, won't you?'

'The Algarve?'

Hooky consulted his wristwatch with an air of great seriousness.

'At this moment, unless the Mafia at Heathrow have decided not to let anybody go anywhere until they get another twenty-five quid a week and freedom to pilfer unhindered, the man you want to interview is high up in the air over France sipping inferior champagne and heading for the Algarve where he proposes to stay for at least three months.'

'Three months!'

'So you'll have to find somebody else to be bitchy about, won't you?'

Peggy Shelton said something extremely uncomplimentary about men in general and Hooky in particular and banged out of the Arms.

Tom Pacey came back to the centre of the stage.

'I take it your friend is a lady-journalist, Mr Hefferman?'

'It's a contradiction in terms,' Hooky told him sourly.

'I didn't know his Lordship was off to foreign parts.'

'He isn't. At this moment he is probably messing about with that cageful of little birds he's so keen on; or trying to persuade the head gardener to start growing the tomatoes underground; or busy about one or the other half-dozen crack-pot ideas he gets hold of. But never mind; it keeps him happy. As far as I know he hasn't the slightest intention of going to the Algarve, Tom; but it's sometimes necessary to drape the harsh outlines of bare fact with the gracefully concealing clothes of fiction. Truth is a very dangerous commodity; if you insist on always telling the truth sooner or later you are going to be found out, and which of us could stand that?'

The main drawing-room at the Hall had at its far end french windows leading into a large Victorian conservatory; for some years past this had been divorced from its original use and converted into an aviary. Charles Fenton had never before in his life taken the slightest notice of small birds, but immediately on taking up residence at the Hall he became enthusiastically enamoured of this new toy and would stand for an hour at a time in the conservatory whilst the budgerigars, the macaws, the canaries, the love-birds, the brilliant Spanish tawlins and the tiny incredible multicoloured forbels were weaving rainbows in the air around him. Probably in three months' time he would have lost all interest in them, but at the moment the aviary was where he was most likely to be found.

He was there when Hooky returned from his brisk, two-rounds encounter with Peggy Shelton.

Charles listened with most of his attention on the little birds, which, although he knew nothing about them, were still fascinating him. Hooky concluded his semi-humorous account and was slightly taken aback by the response it provoked.

'I suppose you had to—'

'Well, isn't that what I'm here for?'

'Funny how you can be scared of a thing and yet in a way still want it – look at that little grey bird with yellow spots, isn't it extraordinary?'

'Fascinating; but I don't care if it's a yellow bird covered with grey spots. I thought you hired me to keep the Press away. What's all this about being scared of a thing and still wanting it?'

'I was thinking of horses. Look at that pair of love-birds. Do you suppose they will mate?'

'Not if they've got any sense, not with the world the way it is. You were thinking of horses?'

'When I was a kid I was made to ride; I was absolutely terrified of it and practically sick with fright for hours beforehand, and yet in a way it fascinated me; in a way I almost wanted to be frightened. It's the same with women; I know I would be scared to death if I met one of those frightful women journalists and yet I can't help thinking it might be rather fun.'

'Treat yourself to another think, Charlie boy. You can take it from me you wouldn't find it even remotely resembling fun if Peggy Shelton had a go at you. She'd tie you up in knots and then fairly crucify you in that page of hers.'

'I suppose you've known plenty of women, Hooky?'

The disarming query took Hooky by surprise and set his thoughts racing. Yes, up and down the world, one way and another (but mostly one way, he reflected wryly), he had indeed known a lot of women – too many: hungry ones; happy ones; the clinging sort; the cloying sort; the turn-me-over-and-beat-me kind; the look-you-level-in-the-eye-and-shoot-as-straight-as-you-can kind.

'A sight too many, Charlie,' he answered, 'a sight too many; half of 'em were no good to me, and the other half tore me to bits, and they were all too damned expensive; but looking back on it all I wouldn't have missed any one of them for the world.' He cast an eye at his host and employer; recently ennobled and enriched. Hooky wondered if he were looking at that rare phenomenon, a man of thirty who was also a virgin. He wondered if Charles had ever lain in a woman's arms. He wondered what would happen to him when he did come up against some dainty rogue in porcelain, when the fatal dark-eyed beauty eventually come on the scene.

'These silly little tawlins keep trying to get out,' Charles said. 'They don't know what's good for them.'

'Faith, they're not the only ones,' Hooky assured him.

Hooky's second encounter with an inquisitive press was even more easily dealt with than his first and was certainly more agreeable. The *Farnbridge Advertiser* was not a paper that rushed things and, moreover, it was one that prided itself on getting its priorities right. There was a great deal of important routine stuff to be dealt with every week: the W.I., the Bowls Club; the Rotary Lunch; the people who reluctantly died; other people who recklessly insisted on getting married. These were all matters which had first claim on the attention of a depleted staff, so that the new occupant of Pentallan Hall had been installed for nearly a fortnight before Henry Capper found his way over to that part of his territory and into the bar of the Pentallan Arms. He saw Tom Pacey in conversation with a stranger, a stranger who looked a useful sort of citizen, one who if life bit him would be more than capable of biting back. Not surprisingly Tom was talking about his great passion, cricket.

Henry Capper might not know Hooky; but Hooky, by instinct, felt pretty sure about him as soon as he came in. Hooky could smell the printer's ink and hear the agonised cry down the blower; 'for Christ's sake, when am I going to have that stuff of yours on the Council Meeting?'

The newcomer's first words confirmed Hooky's guess.

'The usual, Tom. What's happening round about? Any news?'

Hooky was a great believer in getting himself into an advantageous strategic position. He forestalled the newcomer's wallet-reaching hand.

'I'm in the chair. Join me, please.'

'That's very handsome of you. Henry Capper, by name.'

'Hefferman.' Hooky pointed to his twice-broken nose. 'Commonly known as Hooky for pretty obvious reasons. Let me make a guess – is it called the *Advertiser,* the *Record,* the *Free Press* or what?'

'The *Advertiser* actually. Are you in the game too?'

'Not really. The fringes only. I pop into El Vino occasionally just to see how the boys are misbehaving themselves and to hear the latest lies.'

'Ah, I never made Fleet Street.'

'Sensible man, London has become a desolation and a howling wilderness.'

Capper gave a short laugh. 'Time was when I wouldn't have minded doing a bit of howling in the wilderness myself, but—' The sentence trailed away, and Hooky supplied what he thought might be a fitting conclusion.

'But you grew wiser?'

'But this stuff beat me.' Capper held up the double Scotch which Tom Pacey had poured out for him and which had already suffered considerable inroads. 'This and – oh, other things. So I lowered my sights a long time ago, and now it's pretty humdrum stuff; boring but undemanding; I can do it on my head. What brings you to these parts? Don't tell me you are the forerunner of a huge international consortium prospecting for oil in mid-Hertfordshire; that would be a story.'

'Sorry to disappoint you,' Hooky laughed. 'Nothing to do with oil. I'm staying for a while at Pentallan Hall.'

'Are you, indeed? Then you can save me a journey. I want a couple of paras about the new man up there. What's he like?'

Hooky shrugged his shoulders. 'What is anybody like?' he countered. 'He's human.'

'Well, that makes a nice change. I sometimes think half the people I write about aren't. Not married, is he?'

'No.'

'Any signs?'

'Not that I know of.'

'No sex orgies up at the Hall, I suppose?'

'I haven't seen any yet; but one lives in hope, of course.'

Capper laughed. 'He sounds harmless and uninteresting enough,' he said.

'That just about hits the mark,' Hooky told him. 'What you

want to say is that the new owner of Pentallan Hall, an eligible bachelor in his early thirties, declares himself delighted with the stately home he has inherited and has already pronounced his intention of living there quietly and taking an unobtrusive part in the life of the local community.'

Capper was lost in admiration. 'You sound as though you might have been on the *Advertiser* for years,' he said. 'That's just the sort of guff they want.' He pushed his empty glass forward, 'What about the other half?'

Whilst Tom Pacey was serving the drinks the door opened and, accompanied by a gust of cold spring wind, the Colonel came in. He gave a quick, brisk nod and barked out a quick, brisk greeting.

'Evening, Tom.'

'Good evening, Colonel.'

The newcomer was so true to type that just as he was, without any make-up or accessories, he could have walked straight on to the stage for any comedy of the twenties; the leather patches on shoulder and at elbows, the short moustache, the clipped sentences, the over-red cheeks, the startlingly blue and rather vacuous eyes – noting all these things Hooky couldn't make up his mind whether nature was imitating art, or art nature.

The Colonel took a quick look at the two men already in the bar and was not particularly interested in them; he addressed himself to the landlord.

'I shall be missing your cricket match, Tom.'

'I'm sorry to hear that, Colonel. We shall be hard up for batting without you. Going away, then, are you?'

'Spain. Six months. Six months sunshine out of these damned east winds. And it's not costing me a penny.'

'I wish I knew the trick of that, Colonel.'

'I've let the cottage. Advertised it in *The Times.* Dolled it up a bit, you know, for the Personal Column. Made it sound pretty nice. Well, of course, it *is* a nice little place. And people read *The Times.* Even today. Can't say I like that fellow Thomson much, but *The Times* is still all right. And anyway, as I say, people still read the Personal Column. Must do. This lady did, anyway. Rang me up straight away. I had hardly started the crossword before she was on the telephone. Sounded just what she wanted and just the area where she wanted to be. Could she come down next day and look at it? Well, I've learnt one thing in life, Tom: never say "no" to the ladies, what? So, dammit, she was down here before lunch and everything fixed up by three o'clock. I've got a six-months let at the figure I wanted, half the rent paid cash down already, and everyone round here has got a most confoundedly attractive lady neighbour.'

CHAPTER FOUR

Dolly was a great believer in the axiom that 'things have got to happen'; she thought, and frequently said, that 'there must be some sort of a plan – if not, nothing makes any sense, does it?' It was a belief reinforced in her every time that she went to consult Madame Vana.

Madame Vana was always saying, in that sibilant mid-European intonation of hers, 'It's all set down, my dear, set down so as you can see it; you see things straight and read them right, you know what's going to happen, don't you? So you know when to be careful and when to be bold.'

Dolly went to see Madame Vana regularly. By now she was very familiar with the dark basement flat in Earls Court. The heavy, dark-red curtains were always drawn; the electric fire was always burning; the atmosphere was always stuffy.

Dolly, who had a passion for cleanliness, disliked the smell of the ill-ventilated room, just as she disliked Madame Vana's greasy hair and unwashed hands, but all the same there was something about the fat, ugly woman that was impressive, frightening almost. There she sat, plump and short of breath, in the middle of her untidy, unsavoury room like a spider. Did she ever go out at all? you wondered. Did she have any connection at all with the outside world? It didn't seem to matter. She claimed to have connection with another world, the invisible world brushing our shoulders all the time, touching our lives at a dozen places every day.

There were times when the eyes set deep in the wrinkled, lined face glazed over, and you had an uncomfortable feeling that they were seeing things close to hand, touching you almost, which you could not see. Christ! you thought. What's happening now?

At those moments Dolly felt scared; every now and again in that stuffy room she was made aware of a strange wind blowing from some larger space; then she would watch, fascinated, whilst the powerful hands with their black nails laid out the Tarot cards and the odd voice croaked, 'Oh, my dear, you must be careful, you really must; careful; there's trouble here; dark things, wrong things; the pattern's going wrong for you.'

But this time it was different.

This time it was encouraging. 'Oh, my dear, things are going to change for you. I can see paper here. Paper is going to mean something to you somehow. The pattern is going to change. When the pattern changes you must change with it, mustn't you? When things come your way you must go along with them, mustn't you? Act on them.'

At the end of the session Dolly laid the customary five-pound note on the brown tablecloth, and for a moment Madame Vana's eyes lost their other-worldly look and became severely practical. The unwashed hands gathered up the money in no uncertain grasp. There were a lot of five-pound notes hidden in the cupboard in the corner.

It was half-past four when Dolly came up the basement steps into the Earls Court Road. The session with Madame Vana had cheered her up. As she went along she kept saying to herself: Of course, it probably means nothing really, but still....

She decided to have a cup of tea before going back to the flat and she turned into the first tea-room that she came to. It was small and at that time of the afternoon crowded; in fact, she could see only one vacant seat and that at a table where a man was already sitting. As Dolly approached he looked up and gave her a quick, impersonal smile as much as to say, 'Yes, please sit here if you want to; I have no objection at all'; he then resumed his study of the typewritten document he had been reading and took no more notice of Dolly.

Waiting for her tea and bun to be brought, Dolly amused

herself by studying the man opposite. Youngish (thirty-two or -three?); intelligent looking; clean; smartly dressed. Stockbroker? Lawyer? Accountant? He might be any of these things, she thought, and then: I wonder if he's part of Madame Vana's new plan for me?

The thought amused her because she felt not the slightest attraction of any sort towards the man, nor after that first quick moment of superficial politeness did he pay the least attention to her.

When he came to the end of the document he had been reading he put it away in a thin, black briefcase, picked up his coat and, without so much as a glance at Dolly, left.

So much for the new pattern of things, Dolly thought. She looked round the crowded tea-room and could see nobody of any interest in it; not for the first time it occurred to her that the human animal at feeding-time was not particularly attractive.

She felt bored and was beginning to regret that the stockbroker-lawyer-accountant had not stayed a little longer; at least it might have been possible to have some casual conversation with him. Then she noticed that on the floor by the seat where he had been sitting he had left behind a newspaper. She bent and picked it up, glad of anything to read. It was *The Times*, a paper which normally she didn't see. The small advertisement columns were the first things that took her attention, and she began to read them, without any particular interest and more for the sake of something to do than for anything else.

Suddenly her attention was caught by a single word, the name of a town: *Farnbridge*. Only a few days before she had read the same name in another paper, in the *Evening Standard*'s account of Lord Pentallan's death in Farnel's. Farnbridge was where young Charlie Fenton (she still thought of him in Maidenhead terms) had inherited a family seat and a family fortune. Now she read the advertisement with sharpened interest and closer attention:

Farnbridge: favourite Herts countryside yet easy distance London: charming modernised cottage; large recep.; 2/3 bed.; mod. kit. etc.; all main services; garden; owner going abroad for six months will let to responsible and sympathetic tenant. Rent by arrangement. Phone (evenings) Farnbridge 262.

Dolly read through this twice, slowly and with growing astonishment mixed even with a little fear. 'I can see paper here,' Madame Vana said. 'Paper is going to mean something to you somehow.'

She called for her bill, paid it and with *The Times* clutched firmly in her hand left the tea-room for Marble Arch.

Bunny was sitting in front of the T.V. set watching racing from Newmarket. If being an inveterate gambler meant making big bets and risking a lot of money, Bunny could not be accused of it, but he had a passion for watching racing and had some small bets – never more than a pound or two – most days.

Dolly had no interest in racing whatsoever. To her it seemed the most boring possible way of losing money, and Bunny's 'dribs and drabs', as she called his cautious bets, the most stupid way of all. She couldn't see any point in having so small a bet that it didn't really matter whether you won or lost. If he had to bet she would have preferred him to bet big and take a genuine risk.

Ever since reading of the good luck that had come the way of Charlie Fenton (or Charlie Pentallan as she must now think of him) Dolly had been wondering how she could introduce herself back into his life. She meant to do it and she was sure it could be done. The question was *how*: how to contrive to pop up again apparently perfectly naturally and without her reappearance being suspected of having been inspired by reports of that one and a quarter million.

Now she thought that chance, fate, 'the pattern', was offering her the ideal way.

There were snags. Chiefly one snag. Money. Money meant

Bunny – Bernard Arthur Daley, ex-public-school boy; ex-Oxford; ex-three years commissioned officer in a good regiment; not exactly cashiered (bad for the regiment's reputation) but very strongly advised to resign because of irregularities in the mess funds; since then established con man with his own particular line of business, extremely clever at putting across the patter and the impersonation but lacking – as Dolly saw it – in ambition and real resolution.

Dolly was already determined to get the six-months' lease of the cottage at Farnbridge, and if there was one principle she had become convinced of in life it was that when you wanted anything you had to pay for it, and if you were able to pay you usually got what you wanted. She had already made up her mind not to haggle over whatever rent was asked for the cottage and to offer to pay at least half of it in advance, cash down. This consideration brought her back to the man she was living with. What money they had he possessed; she had none. She was not at all sure that she wanted him to have any part in whatever game she was going to play; in fact, she had practically made up her mind that she didn't want him. More and more she was realising that Bunny was a small-time man and would go on being a small-time man and that she would be better off without him, free to play the hand her own way and to shape her own life.

But at the moment she needed him for working capital.

At her entry into the room he leant forward and switched off the television.

'Would you believe it! Three seconds. The first three races. One after the other. My horse beaten less than a length each time. Just my luck!'

'If you always have bad luck at it why don't you give this stupid betting business up?'

'What's the harm in it? I've only lost three quid this afternoon.'

'I can't think why you bother piddling about with peanuts like that. What's the point in winning or losing three quid?'

'If they had all three won it wouldn't have been only three quid.'

'If, if, if – your life is full of ifs, Bunny, one long if after another.'

'Whose life isn't?'

'Christ, don't turn philosopher as well as racing tipster; that I couldn't stand.'

Bunny always preferred peace to war (it was one of the traits about him which irritated the woman) and he sought to turn the conversation by asking, 'And what have you been up to?'

'Reading *The Times.*'

'Reading *The Times*?'

She pushed the paper forward for his attention, a pointed fingernail indicating the entry she wanted him to read.

He read it and looked up for enlightenment.

'Farnbridge,' Dolly emphasized.

'What happens at Farnbridge?' he asked.

'It's near Pentallan Hall.'

Although he didn't yet know what she was driving at, the word struck an echo in his memory.

'Pentallan? Wasn't it Lord Pentallan who had a fit or heart attack or something in Farnel's the other day and died in the Club?'

Dolly nodded. 'And his heir Charlie Pentallan has come in for the family plus a million and a quarter.'

'Nice work if you can get it.'

'I used to know Charlie Pentallan; Charlie Fenton he was in those days.'

'You did?'

'And I propose to get to know him again.'

Bunny smiled. He began to see daylight. Trust Dolly, he thought, to put him on to a good thing. He had forgotten the flare-up between them after his failure at Dalesford and it didn't enter his head that she might be thinking of doing something on her own. His ingenious mind began to see all sorts of possibilities: Dolly established on a friendly footing –

'How simply marvellous to meet up again after all this time', and so on; then Dolly's prosperous, high-powered, executive brother just over from Australia (or possibly Canada – the accent was easier) with golden opportunities for anyone with a little cash to spare – oil possibly, off the Newfoundland coast; or bring in the word 'Alaska' somehow, Alaska sounded big and untapped and promising; Alaska Developments Inc. – something like that.

'We might be on to something there, Dolly.'

She let the 'we' go unquestioned.

'I want to get the lease of this cottage for six months and get established there.'

'Of course you do.'

'So I want money for the rent.'

'You haven't signed the lease yet? How much is it likely to be?'

'I suppose twenty-five or thirty a week. Say thirty. That's seven-eighty for the six months. I want to be able to put half that, well three-fifty anyway, down on the table, *plonk*, and say, "here's three months' rent in advance. Now will you let me have the place?"'

Bunny nodded slowly.

'And whilst I'm there I've got to live.'

'We've both got to live.'

'You're not coming, Bunny.'

'Not to start with; no, of course not; not to start with; but I'll be there as soon as you want me. Don't you worry, I'll be there.'

She made no comment on that and returned to her main theme.

'So what I want is money. Now. I want a thousand.'

'God Almighty, that will clean me right out. The most I can do is five hundred.'

'You'll find a way of making some more. I want that five hundred now and I shall want some more later on.'

The Colonel had six telephone calls in response to his advertisement in *The Times*. Two were exploratory and indecisive (what the Colonel himself called 'wimble-wamble'); two didn't want as long a let as six months; two sounded genuinely interested, and one of them asked if she might come down the following morning to see the property.

She arrived by eleven o'clock, and the Colonel took to her at once. Like many men who like to think of themselves as 'men of the world' he was astonishingly gullible, and Mrs Acton (as Dolly was now calling herself) took him in from the word go.

The Colonel considered himself as 'a man for the ladies' yet, oddly enough, his taste in women was inclined towards the masculine ones. He thought Mrs Acton sensible, downright, business-like and 'a damned good-looker', and by the time that she enthusiastically agreed to sit down and have a mid-morning glass of sherry with him he was already congratulating himself on having found the right sort of tenant. There remained only the matter of the rent, and although the Colonel was as fond of money as most people he was sufficiently old-fashioned to feel some diffidence in discussing it with a lady.

To his relief Mrs Acton herself broached the subject, thus confirming his opinion of what a sensible, practical sort of person she was.

'And what about the rent, Colonel?' Dolly asked.

'The rent? Yes, indeed, one has to consider that, of course. I'm not really used to this sort of thing but – er – I was thinking in terms of, well, say – er – thirty pounds a week?'

This suggestion was put forward tentatively, the question mark at the end of it being clearly audible as much as to say that if thirty pounds a week sounded a bit steep there was always room for negotiation. To the Colonel's relief Mrs Acton didn't want to negotiate.

'Thirty?' she said briskly. 'Yes, that's all right; I can manage that.' (What a sensible person she is, the Colonel thought.)

'I expect you would like something in advance, wouldn't you?'

'Well—'

'You see, Colonel, the lease of my London flat has come to an end and I badly want to have a *pied-à-terre* somewhere for a few months anyway to give me time to look round. I like Gorse Cottage and I am sure I shall be happy here whilst I am looking for something more permanent. As I say, I can manage thirty pounds a week rent – just' (she made a humorous grimace to indicate that, like all other gentlefolk, she was finding the modern world pretty difficult money-wise) 'and I am quite prepared to pay something considerable in advance now – say, two hundred pounds – if we can get the lease and all the legal side of it settled straight away.'

The Colonel said it was a pleasure to do business with her but three hundred in advance was more what he had been thinking of: 'My legal chap is in Farnbridge,' he explained. 'We can call and see him straight away today and, once we are settled, then you can move in almost at once – say, in two days' time. I'm sure you will like it here; there are plenty of nice people around.'

Dolly, of course, did not make the mistake of asking then and there about Pentallan Hall. She waited until she had been established in Gorse Cottage for some days and the Colonel was safely out of the way in sunny Spain (actually it rained continuously for the first two weeks he was there); then on a shopping expedition in Farnbridge Dolly took herself into W. H. Smith and bought a 2½-inch Ordnance map of the district.

When she opened it up and studied it back in Gorse Cottage she realised that she was in luck; Gorse Cottage stood in Long Wood Lane; barely a quarter of a mile from the cottage there was a turning off the Lane (she had, in fact, already noticed it) marked simply 'the Trackway'; whether this was its name or a description of it wasn't clear, but after a short distance 'the Trackway' ran alongside Pentallan Great Wood, and not far on the other side of Pentallan Great Wood was clearly marked 'Pentallan Hall'. She was within a mile of her target. When she realised that Dolly smiled. 'It's a good sign,' she thought. 'I'm in luck.'

She knew she was even luckier the following day when she saw two men in the middle of Pentallan Great Wood. After lunch she had walked up the Lane for a quarter of a mile and then turned right-handed up the Trackway. This proved to be a rutted, grassy track, clearly not much used, which after a short distance began to be shielded on the left-hand side by a line of good beech trees, the outriders, as it were, of Pentallan Great Wood. Presently a small wooden sign marked 'Footpath' came in sight; it pointed to an easily visible path running between the trees into the wood, and after a moment's hesitation Dolly decided to take it.

She was so essentially a city animal that the silence of the place, the big sentinel trees on every side and the loneliness of it scared her slightly, but she decided to push on and see what happened.

What happened was that the path led her into a clearing, a space roughly circular in shape where for some reason or other trees had either not been planted or had failed to grow and where rough grass and a tangle of brambles had taken over. On the edge of this clearing a large beech had years ago been blown down in some forgotten storm and the rotting bole lay half-covered by grass and ferns.

Close by the fallen tree – one of them was in fact actually sitting on it – were two men. Dolly saw them before they were aware of her and it was then that she knew her luck to be still holding. She recognised Charlie Fenton at once. He was slightly plumper both in face and form, but there was no significant difference between the figure she now saw sitting in a splash of sunlight in the middle of Pentallan Great Wood and the gauche young man who had walked with her on Thames-side at Maidenhead.

The other man, standing by Charlie, talking to him, looked a very different sort of fish – a friend or relation presumably. Like most highly sexed women Dolly had an extremely sensitive early-warning system where men were concerned and she was immediately aware of masculine personality-waves coming from the stranger.

Moving forward she made some slight noise among the dead, dry leaves, and both men looked towards her. She walked up to them slowly, wondering, with inward amusement, whether Charlie would recognise her; she didn't think that he would.

'Can you tell me where this footpath goes to, please?' she led off, adding with splendidly simulated surprise and before either of them could answer her query, 'Why, it's Charlie Fenton, isn't it?'

Young Lord Pentallan rose to his feet and looked at her more closely, memory beginning to stir.

'Did Jonah get married successfully?' she prompted. 'Maidenhead. Do you remember? Oh, years ago!'

Charlie began to smile. 'Maidenhead! Good heavens, yes. In that pub on the river where we had Jonah's bachelor dinner. Dolly, isn't it? I'm sure it is. Dolly.'

'Quite right. How clever of you to remember,' she smiled encouragingly at him. 'Dolly Acton now.'

'And what on earth brings you here in the middle of Pentallan Wood?'

The other man then spoke for the first time.

'Are you by any chance connected with Fleet Street, Miss Acton?'

'*Mrs* Acton; and Fleet Street? I don't know what you mean.'

'I mean *Women and Fireside, Woman's Outlook, Wife and Home, Mrs and Miss* and half a dozen other weeklies any of which would pay handsomely for fifteen hundred words and a photograph on eligible bachelors of the English countryside. If you want to interview Lord Pentallan you had better have a chat with me first.'

Charlie's guardian angel, Dolly thought; some angel by the look of him; pretty difficult to flannel, but no sense in falling foul of him – yet. She smiled agreeably.

'I'm afraid I haven't the faintest idea what you are talking about. And who is Lord Pentallan anyway?'

‘I am,’ Charlie chipped in quickly. ‘My uncle died just recently, and I came into the title.’

‘Congratulations. Lord Pentallan? Good heavens, so this wood belongs to you, does it?’

‘It seems to be part of the estate, yes.’

‘Then I’m trespassing. I am very sorry, Charlie – am I still allowed to say Charlie?’

‘Of course. Yes. Please do. And actually I’m not sure that you are trespassing. This may well be a public footpath; I haven’t found out all the details of the property yet. What brings you here, anyway?’

‘I’ve taken the tenancy of a cottage in Long Wood Lane from an old friend of mine, Colonel Fellows; it’s about a mile away.’

‘So we are neighbours?’

‘I had no idea I was going to be so lucky, Charlie.’

‘You must come over to the Hall and have a drink or a meal some time.’

‘I should simply love to.’

‘I’ll fix it up one day soon,’ Charlie promised.

CHAPTER FIVE

After the first few days of settling in Dolly discovered, rather to her surprise, that she was actually enjoying the business of living at Gorse Cottage.

She had often declared, and declared vehemently, that London was the only place to live in and that she simply couldn't imagine existence anywhere else; and this was still an article of faith with her. Of course, she would be going back to London to live permanently, she was still quite clear on *that* point; but meanwhile there was no sense in not enjoying what she looked upon as her holiday in the country, especially as it was a holiday that she hoped would prove extremely profitable.

She was in no hurry to decide on a definite plan. For all his admitted ability at the con game, Bunny had never had a fish on the line worth a million and a quarter. Dolly was convinced that she was engaged in a game well worth playing and she had no intention of spoiling things by hurrying.

Gorse Cottage was a neat, compact little house where Colonel Fellows had obviously developed to a high degree the regular soldier's genius for making himself comfortable; foremost among his assets in that direction was Mrs Penny, a treasure of a daily woman who arrived by bicycle at ten o'clock every morning and theoretically should have left at twelve but she quite often stayed on for an extra half-hour. Mrs Penny did all the housework (the place was as clean and shining as a new pin), prepared and nearly always cooked the lunch, and frequently made half the preparations for the evening meal as well.

The kitchen was conveniently small; standing in the middle

of it Dolly could get at everything she wanted merely by reaching for it and without having to move; it boasted an electric cooker (which she preferred to the gas one in the Marble Arch flat), a refrigerator and – a thing she was delighted to find – a small deep-freezer.

Getting meals in the Marble Arch flat had been a bore but, here in Gorse Cottage, Dolly was finding that fixing up something for herself in the evening, without being under any pressure about it, without having to bother whether it was going to be approved or not, was really rather good fun. She was glad to be away from Bunny for a while; that was the truth of it, she had to admit to herself. Of course, Bunny was a first-rate confidence-man, no doubt about that, and he might have to be brought into whatever scheme was ultimately thought up. But he didn't have to be brought in yet. Six months gave her plenty of time to make up plans, and making up plans was fun.

The chance encounter in Pentallan Great Wood could hardly have gone better from her point of view. Charlie had seemed genuinely pleased to see her and hadn't shown the slightest sign of suspicion about her presence there. She remembered him from the Maidenhead evening as a lightweight, somebody she could twist round her little finger if she wanted to, and he didn't seem to have altered much. The toughie with him was a very different proposition. Dolly met him again more formally when, in response to a telephone invitation, she went up to the Hall for a drink some days after that first meeting.

'... And this is Mr Hefferman, Hooky to his friends.'

'I hope that includes me.' Dolly switched on her most feminine smile for Hooky's benefit, but she wasn't at all sure that it would have much effect on him; he looked as though a lot of women had smiled at him in his time.

'Hooky's staying down here for a while to scare off intruders,' Charlie said.

'Intruders! Oh dear, I hope that *doesn't* include me, trespassing in your wood!'

'Good heavens, no, Dolly, of course not; you are welcome to walk wherever you like all over the property. I hardly know the footpaths myself yet. But there was a certain amount of publicity owing to the way my uncle collapsed and died in his club – perhaps you saw about it in the papers?'

'Collapsed in his club? No, I didn't see a thing about it. How frightfully sad for you.'

The new Lord Pentallan gave a high-pitched nervous laugh, a thing he was wont to do at unexpected and, often enough, inappropriate moments.

'Not really. I scarcely knew the old boy, and I don't think he liked me much anyway; but, of course, he couldn't prevent the estate and so on coming to me; and since he wasn't exactly a pauper I've no objection to that at all; but, as I say, there was a certain amount of publicity just at first – beastly press photographers and so on – and Hooky's staying with me to fend all that off.'

'I shouldn't think you'll be worried down here,' Dolly said, 'and anyway I'm quite sure Mr Hefferman will look after you.'

'Hooky to you,' Hooky said, 'and I'll do my best. What about drinks – shall I see to them, Charlie?'

Dolly watched Hooky pouring out the drinks with interest. He didn't go in for 'dribs and drabs' like Bunny did. This was an altogether tougher egg than Bunny; he had an edge on him. It would be more convenient when he was out of the way, of course, but Dolly was a woman and it was difficult for any woman to want Hooky out of the way altogether. Perhaps in time Charlie could be persuaded to get rid of him, she thought. She could foresee a lot of fun in developing her scheme; the possibilities in it were opening up intriguingly.

When Dolly had left after that first visit Hooky, helping himself to a final large drink, asked about her. Charlie once more gave an account of the stag party at Maidenhead. 'That's twelve years ago,' he said. 'I can't imagine how it's all gone so quickly. I was only just eighteen.'

'We were all eighteen once,' Hooky assured him, 'though

every morning when I'm shaving I'm inclined to doubt it. The important thing is not to remain eighteen.'

'I should have thought exactly the opposite: stay eighteen for as long as you can.'

'Too bloody vulnerable. When you're eighteen you don't know how to deal with tigers, and one way and another there are plenty of them about. What happened to Jonah?'

'Oh, he got married, of course. Quite an occasion. You know the sort of thing. Champers galore and telegrams and speeches. I haven't seen him for years. I suppose he is – well, just a married man. Have you ever thought of marrying, Hooky?'

'We all have mental aberrations at times. I've been dangerously near it once or twice, but in the end the girls had more sense. What about you?'

Charlie Pentallan gave his sudden, distracting laugh, and not for the first time Hooky wondered whether his employer was a homosexual.

'You never know,' Charlie answered archly with deliberate vagueness.

'Well, watch your step, that's all,' Hooky advised him. 'If there's any jam about, a hell of a lot of flies will come buzzing after it, believe me; and now and again there'll be a wasp among them.'

When he was halfway through his third week at the Hall Hooky's conscience – which usually had to fight against pretty heavy odds – began to worry him. It was clear that, as far as the Press was concerned, the Pentallan scent was dead cold. The questing hounds had already been called off on to more headline-worthy stories; what with rape, incest, and child-beating, to say nothing of football managers demanding twice as much salary as the Prime Minister and overrated film actors declaring their undying love for the fifth time the decent, home-loving, smugly virtuous British Public had plenty to read about.

All Hooky's instincts told him that Fleet Street had lost interest in Charlie Pentallan; in a day or so, he made up his mind, he would in honesty have to explain this to his employer and reluctantly take his leave.

Reluctantly because the *dolce far niente* charm had not yet worn off. In an agreeable, soporific way he was finding life at Pentallan Hall good; Skipton was surely the doyen of menservants, and Mrs Skipton, invisibly immured in the kitchen, was a magnificent cook. Every morning after a leisurely breakfast Hooky amused himself trying to thread the intricacies of the famous yew-hedge maze, the centrepiece of a garden which in its hey-day, when there were six full-time men to look after it, had been renowned.

Most evenings, sometime between six and seven, he was able to pay a visit to the Pentallan Arms. At that hour the long, low bar seldom held more than a couple of other people and it was possible to have desultory, easy-going conversations with Tom Pacey. Like all village publicans Tom was a great clearing-house of local information, but like all fanatics he was difficult to steer away from his pet subject. Not for the first time he was bewailing to Hooky what effect the Colonel's absence in Spain was going to have on 'my cricket match'.

'What is this famous match of yours, Tom? Is it an annual event, or what? Tell me about it.'

'Ah, well, sir, not being a Pentallan man you wouldn't know about it; but, if I may say so, it is *the* annual event for the village. It's the old Thirty-second, you see.'

'Mix me another Pimms, Tom, and stop talking in riddles. What the devil is the old Thirty-second?'

Honest Tom's eyes opened wide in astonished reproach for such ignorance.

'Why, Mr Hefferman, the regiment, of course. The 32nd Hussars, my old mob. The P. and L.s, they're known as in the Service.'

'P. and L.s?'

'The poke 'em and leave 'em lot. Just a nickname, sir; a bit slanderous really; they didn't always leave them. In my time they had a really good cricket team. The Colonel was as keen as mustard. My word, how he hated the modern set-up, all these chaps after every penny they can screw out of the game and giving themselves airs in the press and on the box and talking about being overworked and all the rest of it. The greatest honour any Englishman can have, the Colonel used to say, next to belonging to the Thirty-second of course, is to play cricket for England.'

'I used to play a bit of cricket myself once,' Hooky said reminiscently.

'You did, sir? Well, you're the right build for it, I must say. Who did you play for?'

'I was in the University side – Oxford – until the Vice-Chancellor decided he didn't want me up there anymore, and then I used to turn out regularly for the Foresters.'

'The Free Foresters? Did you really? Then you're a class player, Mr Hefferman. What did you do, bat or bowl?'

'They used to send me in first to open the batting, the theory being to put the numskulls in front to take the edge off the fast bowlers and let the good players come in later when the attack was blunted a bit.'

'Ah, you don't fool me,' Tom Pacey laughed. 'If you went in number one for a side like the Free Foresters, you must have been good, Mr Hefferman. Any chance of your playing for my side this summer?'

'What exactly is your side, Tom? You get up a village team to play your old regiment, is that it?'

'That's exactly it, sir. We make a regular week-end of it; the gardens up at the Hall are on show, especially that funny old maze up there; there's an exhibition in the Church Hall, old things connected with the village from the past and so on; and, of course, the cricket match itself. The Thirty-second have still got a good team; they come down in a couple of coaches, wives and kids and the lot; and, my word, don't they just about drink some beer; but they've never beaten us at cricket yet. No, never. I've always managed to get a good side together; to start with, some of the village lads are pretty useful, and then getting the Colonel to play was a real bonus.

Good enough to play for a county the Colonel is; worth fifty on the board every time he bats. What he wants to go off to Spain for with the summer coming on I can't imagine. He won't get any cricket there.'

'Well, for one thing he has been clever enough to let his cottage to a charming lady – she is a charming lady, isn't she, Tom?'

In the course of being a publican Tom Pacey had learnt a number of things, when not to express an opinion being perhaps the most valuable of them.

'Mrs Acton by name, sir, as I understand,' he answered very correctly. 'The lady has been in here a couple of times for a quiet drink and, of course, I have been very pleased to see her. Very pleased to see anybody in the Arms, sir. And now can I count on you to turn out for me in the match, Mr Hefferman? June the second it will be this year.'

Hooky sighed slightly. Old memories stirred within him. Old, sweet memories. The Parks in bright, spring sunshine. The marvellous sound of the full meat of the bat meeting the red round of leather fair and square – just right; the resigned look on the face of cover-point as meteor-like the ball sped past him to the boundary; the reassuring *crack* as it hit up against the boundary fence; long, lazy, summer afternoons on village greens with the shadows gradually lengthening and the white figures moving ballet-like across the grass; the panic feeling that had to be fought down the first time that he had set out from the pavilion at Lords on the interminable long walk to the middle; the relief that he didn't have to walk straight back again; the triumph when he did finally come back with a respectable score to his name and a chorus of 'Well played, sir' from the *cognoscenti.*

'You're tempting me, Tom.'

'I wouldn't like to think I was doing that, sir.'

'And you know what Oscar Wilde said about temptation.'

'Wilde, sir? Who did he play for?'

'The Odds and Sods. But he got caught out in the end. Yes, dammit, I'll play for you.'

'Mr Hefferman, you're a gentleman.'

'In these days, Tom, that's almost an insult.'

In the Marble Arch flat tea-time had somehow never seemed of any importance; certainly not of any pleasurable importance; four o'clock was merely a step on the way to the drink hour; but Dolly had already discovered that in the country things were different. Time had a different quality and the day a different flavour. Tea and hot buttered toast at half-past four in the small, comfortable, chintzy drawing-room, in front of a wood fire if the afternoon was growing chilly, had already become one of the delights of Gorse Cottage for her. It was also obviously very much to the liking of Gloriana, a small, almost certainly demon-possessed Abyssinian kitten which Mrs Penny had introduced on the scene. Gloriana was a chocolate-coloured scrap of incredible vitality, of fiendish ingenuity and of devastating charm who had made an entry into Gorse Cottage like a prima donna taking the stage and from the start had manifestly considered the whole place to be hers and hers alone.

Dolly had just provided a saucer of milk for Gloriana and was about to pour out a cup of tea for herself when the front-door bell rang. She put down the tea-pot and went to see who it was.

'I do hope I'm not disturbing you,' Charlie said.

'Good heavens, no.' In point of fact Dolly had had to make an instantaneous mental readjustment. On her way from fireside to front door she had made up her mind that her visitor would be the tough fellow. She had a feeling that where women were concerned Hooky was the sort of character who would always be willing to try his luck; it might have been amusing if he had come to try it, she reflected, but meanwhile she was more than pleased to see Charlie Pentallan, it opened up all sorts of possibilities.

'I happened to be going by the cottage. I just thought you might be in.'

Dolly smiled; she didn't think for one moment that Charlie

had 'happened to be going by'; she thought that he had walked over especially to see her.

'Well, here I am,' she answered. 'Just about to have tea. Won't you join me?'

Another cup and saucer were produced, and luckily there was a cake in Dolly's small store-cupboard. Gloriana showed her approval of the visitor by settling happily on his lap. Sitting there, in front of the not altogether necessary yet welcome fire, comfortably ensconced on the chintz-covered sofa, tea-cup in hand, Charlie Pentallan was the perfect picture of the male animal enjoying being looked after. Dolly eyed him with amusement; she was good at looking after men when it suited her to do so.

'And where's your faithful bodyguard today?' she asked.

Charlie flushed slightly. 'He's not exactly my bodyguard, you know. Of course, just at first the newspaper people were a nuisance – those dreadful photographers! – and I must admit that Hooky was very useful then.' He took a sip of his tea and added complacently, 'But I expect I should have coped all right by myself really.'

Would you, indeed? the woman thought, but she nodded bright encouragement. 'I'm sure you would have done, Charlie.'

'Actually it's rather a relief not to have him around all the time, to be able to get away on my own occasionally.'

'When you feel like that, you can always come over here, can't you?'

'That's very kind of you, Mrs Acton.' Charlie hesitated a moment or two and then, very daringly for him, went on, 'Of course, you weren't Mrs Acton when we first met that time at Maidenhead, were you?'

Dolly laughed and did a bit of quick thinking. She reckoned she could safely knock a couple of years off her age. 'Indeed, I wasn't. I was barely twenty-one then. Very unsophisticated. You must have thought me very youthful, Charlie.'

'Actually I thought you were pretty wonderful really.'

'Charlie, what a nice thing to say!'

'And how long have you been Mrs Acton?'

Dolly's choice of a name under which to masquerade at Gorse Cottage had been entirely fortuitous. It happened that the little shop round the corner which supplied the morning paper to the Marble Arch flat was called 'Acton's' and the name had seemed to her as good as any other. In her mind she had roughly sketched out a past for herself in case personal histories should ever be required and now seemed to be the appropriate moment to elaborate on it a little.

'I was married seven – no, eight – years ago, Charlie. Four years after the Maidenhead evening.'

'If I had known, I would have sent you a wedding present.'

'Sweet of you. But I'm glad you didn't. It all ended in tears as they say. Partly my fault, I suppose.'

'What happened?'

Dolly spread her hands and gave a little sigh. She was enjoying herself. She doubted whether Bunny could have spun the *spiel* any better.

'What does happen? No good going into all the details. Call it incompatibility if you like. I didn't like the way he behaved, and he obviously must have got tired of anything I could give him. Anyway, after three pretty stormy years he just walked out on me.'

'Your husband deserted you?'

Dolly laughed. 'Don't sound so horrified, Charlie boy. It happens, you know. And, in any case, I'm not trying to make a great tragedy out of it. Yes, he just walked off; "deserted" is the technical term if you want to use it.'

'So are you divorced now?'

'No. I haven't bothered. I can get a divorce any time I want, of course, on grounds of desertion; but, as I say, I haven't bothered yet. So I'm still technically Mrs Acton, of course—' She broke off and gazed reflectively into the fire. Watching her performance that afternoon an interested observer might have been led to wonder why she hadn't done better in her acting career.

'Of course what?' Charlie prompted after a moment.

'Well, you know, living alone isn't all fun by any means, especially for a woman. You tend to get left out of things a bit; and all sorts of problems crop up which you want to talk over and get advice about – but you are a man of the world, I'm sure you understand all that; and I certainly don't intend to inflict my worries on you, that's the most boring thing anybody can do; and nobody has ever accused me of being a bore.'

'I'm sure they haven't, Dolly – I may say "Dolly", mayn't I?'

'Of course you can, you silly boy; it takes me back twelve years to hear you say it and I like that.'

'I didn't think you were a bore that evening, Dolly; I thought you were absolutely smashing.'

'It was fun, wasn't it?'

'*I* thought so,' Charlie Pentallan said.

'Another piece of cake, Charlie?'

Charlie watched approvingly whilst a second generous slice of cake was cut for him.

'Mrs Skipton's a marvellous cook in most ways,' he said, 'but she can't make cakes. Unfortunately she thinks she can and one has to eat the result and pretend to like it.'

'Poor Charlie!' Dolly mocked him.

'Oh, I know I'm lucky—'

'Lucky! I should think you are, with a place like Pentallan Hall to live in and with a couple like the Skiptons to look after you. When we first met weren't you up at Oxford?'

'Yes—'

'Wait a moment. You told me at the time and I'm sure I can remember – Worcester College, wasn't it?'

Charlie nodded delighted. 'Yes, Worcester. How clever of you to remember.'

'I'm good at remembering things when I'm interested. And what happened after Worcester College, Charlie?'

'I got a job in the City. Nine till five. Commuter stuff. Pretty humdrum.'

'In the City? I expect you know all about stocks and shares

and investments and take-over bids and so on, then. Lucky you. Ben – that was the man I married – Ben was very shrewd, too. That was one thing he *was* good at. I never had much money, of course; but if ever I wanted any advice about what shares to buy or how to invest what little I had got I could always ask Ben. Now there's nobody. As I said a moment ago, that's one of the snags of living on your own.'

'If I could ever be of any help—'

'I wouldn't dream of worrying you, Charlie. I'm just so pleased at having picked up an old friendship again.'

When tea was finished and Charlie finally said that he must be getting back, Dolly teased him with 'Your strong-arm man will be wondering where you've got to. He'll be thinking you're in trouble of some sort.'

For a moment Charlie flared up in his characteristic quick manner.

'Hooky's just a friend,' he said. 'I don't need a strong-arm man to look after me. I don't need anyone to look after me.'

'Of course you don't, Charlie,' the woman agreed soothingly, 'and, anyway, when you are tired of having him around you can always say so, can't you?'

Later that evening, sitting in front of the fire with a drink in her hand and thinking over the tea-time *tête-à-tête*, Dolly discovered to her astonishment that her feelings were considerably mixed. Good, useful ground-bait had been laid, and nobody – not even Bunny – could have laid it better. She was sure of that; yet....

She took a sip at her drink and her thoughts ran on their unexpected way: ... yet she was glad that Bunny wasn't there; this pigeon was going to be altogether too easy, too ripe for plucking.

She rose from the low stool on which she was sitting and moved quickly across the room. God damn it, she thought in some bewilderment. What's happening to me? I'm not altogether sure that I want to pluck him.

CHAPTER SIX

'I shan't be in to tea this afternoon,' Charlie said, 'but of course Skipton will look after you.'

'You've got a treasure in Skipton,' Hooky answered. 'Gorse Cottage?'

'What if I am going to Gorse Cottage?' The tone of voice was sharp and angry.

By now Hooky had become used to the sudden flare-ups of temper of which his employer was capable and had learnt to pay very little attention to them; his feelings towards the young man alternated between annoyance at his arrogance and apprehension for such vulnerable innocence.

He smiled amiably. 'How's your Chinese?' he enquired.

'My Chinese?'

'There's a wise old bird called Chu Ling; full of good sayings. "He who goes often into the jungle will one day meet a tiger" is one of them.'

'You don't approve of Mrs Acton, do you?'

Hooky genuinely didn't know what to answer to that question; but instinct warned him that on the whole life at Pentallan would be simpler without Dolly Acton in Gorse Cottage.

'Approve? I've approved of too many women in my time and believe me, Charlie boy, it gets dangerous.'

'Her husband treated her very badly. He deserted her, just walked away out of her life one day.'

'He ought to join the Thirty-second.'

'What on earth are you talking about?'

'Tom Pacey's old lot. They've got a nickname—'

'What nickname?'

'I forget it,' Hooky lied, suddenly realising that what would have gone down with the soaks in El Vino might not be appropriate here.

'You really do say some most extraordinary things,' Lord Pentallan complained, his voice rising again to a high note of sudden petulance. 'You may not like Mrs Acton, but I'm afraid I have to tell you, Hooky, that she isn't particularly fond of you either.'

'Why should she be? Why should she be?' The rest of Hooky's thought – after all, I haven't got a title and a million and a bit in the bank – he kept to himself, unuttered; he genuinely didn't know whether it was fair to say it or not.

This slight touchiness between them over the business of tea at Gorse Cottage was nothing unusual; indeed, it was a good deal milder than many of the temperamental storms that were wont to blow up out of nothing. Charlie Pentallan had a genius for flying off the handle, almost screaming for a couple of sentences in that high-pitched voice of his, at the slightest notice and generally without any real cause. On more than one such occasion he had virtually dismissed Hooky; but each time, within minutes, he had been almost on his knees begging him to stay. After there had been one of these incidents Charlie invariably talked it over in Gorse Cottage – 'So I said ... then I said.... I don't see why I should'; the I,I,Is proliferated in the indignant narrative like poles in a Kentish hop-field.

Dolly always listened to him sympathetically and carefully, or at any rate appeared to be so doing; a long time ago she had learnt how to deal with self-pitying males from Mavis Toller, her companion in the care-free barnstorming days. 'Sit still and say nothing' was the advice Mavis gave. 'Just listen. It doesn't matter a damn what you are thinking about; don't have to say a thing yourself. Just let him ramble on about himself and his troubles and any man will think you are the best conversationalist in the world. Half the time my man of the moment was telling me about his soul and how badly he was misunderstood and treated by his wife. I used to be saying the lines of my current part over to myself, but the poor fish never knew. . . .'

When the talk was about Hooky and the latest incident, real or imagined, between him and his employer, Dolly always paid attention. Hooky might be better out of the way; but she very soon learnt that caution was necessary in dealing with Charlie Fenton. You ventured to agree with some vehemently expressed opinion in one sentence only to hear it almost as vehemently denied in the next.

'If he is really such a nuisance you can always get rid of him, can't you, Charlie? Send him away.'

'But I don't want to send him away.'

'Oh – I thought—'

'He's a friend; he's someone to talk to.'

'But from what you said—'

'What did I say?'

'Nothing, Charlie, nothing. Why shouldn't you do just what you feel inclined to? If you feel you still want Hooky Hefferman around, you keep him around. And I expect he's useful in other ways too, besides being a guard, isn't he?'

'What ways?'

'Well, I suppose you can ask his advice about money and so on.'

'I never have. No, I've never asked him about that sort of thing. Of course when my uncle died—'

'*I* don't want to hear about your money, Charlie.'

'No, but I want to tell you. You don't mind if I talk things over with you, do you?'

'Of course not, you silly boy.'

'You've told me before I can come over here and say anything I like.'

'So you can; you know that.'

'You see, I've not been able to do that before, not with a woman. I've never been much good with women. Actually I've never—' Whatever Charles Pentallan was going to say, he hesitated, changed his mind and instead went on: 'I've always been a bit embarrassed with women – shy, I suppose you would call it – until I met you again, that is. Well, actually' – he gave a nervous little laugh – 'I still am shy; a bit; but I'm getting over it.'

'You needn't be shy, Charlie. So you don't go to Hooky for advice about your money?'

He shook his head. 'And, as I was starting to tell you, there's lots of it. When my uncle fell down dead in that dreary old club of his he left an awful lot of money. Of course, he had his lawyers and accountants – dozens of them it seems like – and they all rather terrify me. I just sign where they tell me to sign and hope for the best.'

'Poor Charles!'

'It sounds as though I'm making a poor mouth over what lots of people would think good fortune, doesn't it? I'm sorry.'

'There you go apologising again,' she laughed at him. 'What you want, Charlie, is a friend, someone who isn't one of your professional lawyers or accountants; just a friend; someone who knows his way about the world and about the City who could give you disinterested advice.'

'Of course that's what I want. I know that.'

'That's what I want too. I don't think strong-arm Hefferman would be much good to us there.'

'I never said he would be, did I?'

'We shall have to find somebody else, Charlie, somebody who really will advise us.'

'It's marvellous having you to talk things over with, Dolly.'

The woman laughed a trifle uneasily.

When Charlie Pentallan had left Gorse Cottage after one of these discussions Dolly would sit smoking in her quick, nervous fashion, mulling over what had been said. Half the time she was amused at the innocence of the man; half the time she was angry with herself for not being more elated at how easy the thing looked like being.

Since being installed in Gorse Cottage she had twice spoken to Bunny on the telephone to report how things were going. He had counselled patience and the slow approach.

'It's the spadework that pays,' he said. 'Get well dug in

first and then I'll think up some crackerjack of a scheme to clean up in a big way. I'm off to the West Country for a fortnight and when I'm back you had better come up to the flat for a day and we can talk things over and get a plan made. All right?'

'Yes, I expect I'll be able to come up.'

'What do you mean, you expect you'll be able to? There's nothing to stop you, is there?'

'No, nothing....'

The suggested visit to the Marble Arch flat was overdue, but Dolly kept on postponing it. Life at Gorse Cottage was proving unexpectedly attractive, and yet there were times when she was badly bored; times when she grew tired of listening to Mrs Penny's gossiping anecdotes about the village, or watching Gloriana's acrobatic capers in pursuit of some invisible, imaginary plaything.

In such a mood one evening after it had rained steadily all day so that she had not stirred from the cottage she suddenly decided that she must get out at all costs and that a visit to the Pentallan Arms would be at least some form of diversion.

When she pushed open the door and went in she was glad to see that the bar was not empty. There were two men there. One she knew, one was a stranger to her.

After the damp, cold day the place was warm and welcoming; she was glad she had come. Hooky greeted her enthusiastically.

'Welcome, Mrs Acton.'

'Dolly to you,' she reminded him. Hooky bore all the signs of a man who was beginning to enjoy his evening and his mood suited her own; she understood men in that mood. Hooky introduced the other man. 'A confrère, a fellow labourer in the vineyard, worthily upholding the glorious traditions of the British Press by daily gathering the grapes of fact and distilling from them the wine of distortion, inaccuracy and spleen – Henry Capper of the *Farnbridge Advertiser*.'

Capper only laughed; he had already learnt to like Hooky.

'Just for that I'll take a drink off you, Hefferman,' he said. 'A double. And I expect the lady will have one, too.'

Dolly was only too willing to have one.

'Are you really a newspaperman?' she asked Hooky.

'No, not really. I had a flirtation with Fleet Street once, a temporary love-affair; but, then, I've had a lot of temporary love-affairs—'

'You astonish me.'

'I'm not like Henry here. Henry is the true professional. Dyed in the wool. He knows it all. Never misses a dateline. Hard-working, hard-drinking, hard-living. Not like me at all; I'm a mere babe in the wood.'

'Some babe,' Dolly laughed. She was already beginning to forget the boredom that had attacked her all day.

Tom Pacey resumed the story that he had been telling when her entry had interrupted him.

'... So this old chap was up on one of these quiz programmes on the box. You know the sort of thing, Mr Hefferman – "are the people who live in Rome called Romantics, Romanies or Romans?" – and a one-hundred-and-twenty-seven-pound washing-machine for a prize if you get it right. Well, this old boy I'm telling you about, he'd never known anything but cricket all his life; been a pro with Sussex, not in the top class maybe, but when the sea-fret came over that ground at Hove he could make the ball do all sorts of awkward things. So the Smart Alec running this quiz thing – all slickness and smarminess, you know the type – he put the ten-thousand-dollar question: "now, what is a geriatric, Billy?" Poor old Billy Cawson had never swallowed a dictionary as they say and being a steadfast sort of a man his mind only ran on one thing really. He thought for a bit and came up with his answer: "A Jerry 'atrick," he said. "Why, I suppose that must be a German who takes three wickets in three balls."'

The three men laughed and Dolly said rather petulantly,

'What on earth are you talking about? I don't understand a word of it.'

'No more cricket, Tom,' Hooky cried. 'Cricket's barred. Ladies present. Mrs Acton doesn't like cricket; and, Lord love us all, why should she? There are more important things in the world than cricket.'

Honest Tom Pacey looked unconvinced; but Dolly laughed. Hooky's mood was a welcome antidote to the blues induced by a rainy day which had confined her to the house. Over the rim of her glass she took a long, assessing look at 'the toughie' as she had mentally christened him. As full of masculinity as they come, was her verdict; and she was in a mood when what she wanted most in a man was masculinity.

It was one of those hilarious evenings, with Hooky in great form and Henry Capper happily playing second fiddle, content to push his glass forward regularly for renewal and to get second-hand glimpses of a world he might once have known. Hooky's talk was bawdy and boisterous, lit every now and again with unexpected bits of wisdom picked up whilst rubbing shoulders with life up and down the world; one moment he was pointing out that the Buddha teaches there is no sin only folly, and the next quoting *in extenso* what the girl, encouragingly but outrageously, said to the soldier. Hooky on the shallowness of things ('It's a three-ply world, my friends'); Hooky uttering the old Whitmanesque whoop of joy in animal existence; Hooky suddenly quoting Proust: 'The only real Paradise is the one we have lost.'

Listening to this last remark Dolly wasn't convinced. There aren't many Paradises you've lost, my friend, she thought.

At one point in the evening Hooky said, 'Charlie Pentallan tells me you provide excellent teas in Gorse Cottage.'

'You should try for yourself some day.'

'I'm not really a tea man.'

She gave him a long, level look and said calmly, 'There are other drinks – and diversions.'

Eventually the time came when Henry Capper decided to

go home. 'Tho' God knows what for,' he said. 'There's nobody there.'

'Are you O.K. to ride that bicycle of yours?' Hooky enquired.

'Perfectly. The less sober I am the more easily I keep my balance. It's a sort of compensating law of nature. Nature is kind to drunks.'

'Thank God someone is kind to us.'

Hooky and the woman stood and watched the red rear-light of the bicycle waver somewhat unsteadily into the darkness.

'I hope they carve it on his tombstone,' Hooky said. ' "Nature is kind to drunks." Come to that, I hope they carve it on mine. Not that I'm going to have one, I intend to—'

'Don't talk about tombstones for goodness' sake,' Dolly interrupted him quickly. 'Death and all that sort of thing, I hate it. Especially this evening.'

'I'm against it, too,' Hooky agreed. 'How are you getting back to the cottage? Have you got a bicycle too?'

Dolly said she had not got a bicycle.

'Broomstick?'

She laughed at that. 'Don't tell me you feel bewitched?'

'I feel that at this time of night you ought not to walk up the dark lane by yourself. It could be dangerous.'

'For me, or the lane?'

'I'll walk back with you.'

'I was hoping you would say that.'

In his bedroom in Pentallan Hall, going through the established routine, arranging the small change from his trouser pocket in a neat pile on the dressing-table, taking off his wristwatch and putting it handy by the side of the bed and so on, Hooky turned over in his mind the events of his twenty minutes' stay in Gorse Cottage. Not that there had been any 'events' really; that was the curious part of it. What's wrong with me? Hooky wondered. Dammit, I must be getting old.

Not often had a woman so blatantly thrown herself at him;

and looking back on things he found it difficult to understand exactly why he had refused the obvious invitation. Perhaps it had been too obvious, he mused; that might have had something to do with it. ('Bread and butter can be one of the nicest foods in the world,' someone had once said to him, 'but you don't want it cut too thick, do you? Doorsteps are off-putting.') But there was something beyond that. Hooky was a great man for instincts, and somewhere at the back of his mind, lurking in the undergrowth of only half-formed thoughts, he heard the faint tinkling of a warning bell; there was a feeling that the whole situation of Charlie Pentallan and himself and the woman at Gorse Cottage, so conveniently arriving out of Charlie's past, had something wrong about it. 'In case there is any sort of involvement, for goodness' sake have the sense not to complicate things further by a typical exhibition of your usual uninhibited animalistic behaviour' had been the message which Hooky's guardian-angel, a being with an almost impossible task, had managed to get through to him.

They had walked together away from the inn along the dark lane. The rain had finally ceased and stars were beginning to show in the clearing sky. The night was turning colder.

The living-room of the cottage was comfortable and intimate; the woman switched on the standard lamp and said, 'There the drinks are, Hooky, on the table by the window. Mix yourself one whilst I get out of these tweeds into something more comfortable. I shan't be long.' There wasn't a hack playwright in Grub Street, Hooky thought, who could have resisted using those exact lines as the introduction to the great seduction-scene; but he poured himself out a drink all the same. No sense in being too abstemious, he thought. Moderation in all things, even in self-restraint.

When Dolly came back into the room Hooky had to admit that the full-length, wine-coloured house-gown she had changed into looked a good deal more *pour le comfort* than the tweeds had done and incidentally was a great deal more revealing.

'I took you at your word,' he said, holding up his glass.

She smiled her bright, hard smile at him. 'Good for you, Hooky. I like a man who can hold his drink.'

Hooky drank a toast to her and to the cottage.

'Nice little place you managed to discover for yourself here,' he complimented her.

'Yes. Wasn't I lucky? Do you believe in fortune-telling, the Tarot cards? No, I can see you don't.'

'The world is such a damned queer place,' Hooky answered, 'that I believe everything is improbable and nothing is impossible. There's philosophy for you.'

'I didn't want philosophy from you, Hooky. Well, I *do* believe in the cards. And it was really extraordinary how it worked out. The woman who read them for me said "paper"; I was going to see a piece of paper that would be of importance for me; and in no time at all, absolutely by accident, when I went into this café place for a cup of tea I picked up a copy of *The Times* a man had left behind by his seat and practically the first thing I saw was the advertisement of this cottage. It sounded exactly what I wanted so I rang the number it gave and got in touch with Colonel Fellows and here I am.'

Hooky stared at her for a moment, thinking. He was blessed, or cursed, with a very tenacious memory and it was now putting in some overtime for him.

'So you didn't know Colonel Fellows before coming to Gorse Cottage?' he asked.

'Never seen or heard of the man before in my life. It just all happened out of the blue, like Madame Vana said it would.'

'I see. Somehow I thought you and the Colonel were old friends.'

'Whatever gave you that idea?'

Hooky shook his head and laughed. 'Goodness knows,' he said, lying in his most convincing style. 'Just an impression I got; I don't know how. The great thing is you are comfortably settled here.'

'Very.' She made a gesture to include the warm, intimate

room. 'It looks comfortable, don't you think?'

'Very.'

'And what about you up at the Hall? Are you getting tired yet of holding the little boy's hand?'

'Charlie Pentallan's all right. He's not as hard-bitten as some, of course; but I don't know that I would count that against him. Rather refreshing in a way. He can be damned irritating at times – but, then, which of us isn't? Those birds of his! He's crazy about them for the moment – canaries, love-birds, budgies, blue birds with yellow spots and yellow birds with blue spots. I'm expected to know the names of them all and to keep telling him how marvellous the beastly little twittering noisy things are. Still, I suppose it's harmless. The truth is that just at the moment he's in love with the novelty of his title, with being Lord Pentallan; and there again I don't know that I blame him for that; it must be quite nice in some ways to be a Lord. Of course, it probably sticks ten per cent on the bill everywhere; on the other hand you probably get ten per cent better service.'

Dolly gave a sudden, loud laugh. 'Wasn't that a marvellous remark the hall porter at the club made when Charlie's uncle fell down in a fit? What was it? "It's not the sort of thing we like to happen at the club." Something like that, wasn't it?'

'I don't suppose he really said it.'

'It said in the paper that he did. I read it myself.'

Hooky looked at her quizzically for a moment, the alarm bells sounding faintly at the back of his consciousness. 'Ah, well, in that case it must be true, mustn't it?' he said at last.

'Not that we want to spend all the evening talking about Charlie Pentallan,' Dolly said, seating herself on the sofa in front of the fire and looking up expectantly at Hooky.

'No, indeed,' Hooky agreed. He consulted his wristwatch in an urgent way as though the idea of time had just occurred to him.

'Good Lord, look at the hour! I must be getting back.'

'You're not going, Hooky?'

'On the whole, yes. I think I must be.'

'But it's all nonsense about the time. You can stay here, as long as you like, you know you can. I want you to stay here, Hooky.'

She stretched out a hand towards him, but Hooky ignored it.

'Sorry, Dolly,' he said, 'no dice. I'm off to my virtuous and downy.'

Reliving that scene as he was undressing. Hooky could see again the hatred that had suddenly flashed out of those hard eyes. By God, she was angry, he thought, and I don't know that I blame her altogether. As Boozey French once said, Hell hath no fury like a woman's corns. The memory of Boozey's misquotation made him laugh for a moment; but he could still hear faint sounds of alarm in his head and on the whole, and on reflection, he wasn't sure that there was much to laugh about really.

CHAPTER SEVEN

Half a dozen rubbish bins stood on the pavement waiting to be emptied, the garbage spilling over from some of them; a discarded and crumpled copy of last night's *Evening News* was blowing about; outside one of the houses a man was investigating inside the bonnet of a car the engine of which was roaring noisily.

At half-past ten in the morning the mews near Marble Arch was not an attractive place; Dolly made her way along it and let herself into the flat. Bunny was sitting in the untidy living-room in his dressing-gown, a cup of coffee before him. Breakfast or elevenses? Dolly wondered, amused at catching him in unusual disarray.

When she came in he looked surprised, almost startled. 'Anything wrong?' he queried.

'Why should there be?'

'Why didn't you phone and let me know you were coming?'

'I did try to get through directly after breakfast, but all the London lines were engaged, so I just caught the train and came.'

'You could have rung yesterday evening.'

'I couldn't actually. Not at any reasonable hour. I was out at the local pub. I only decided to come up during the night.'

'Why so suddenly? Like I said, is there anything wrong?'

Dolly laughed; she was beginning to enjoy herself; she had not seen a dropped handkerchief or a smear of lipstick anywhere, none of the standard 'give-aways' beloved of the conventional dramatist, yet the infallible instinct which the female of the species has in these matters made her suddenly sure that Bunny had a woman in the bedroom.

'There's nothing wrong at Farnbridge,' she assured him. 'Is everything O.K. here?'

'Of course it is. Why shouldn't it be?'

Dolly was examining her own feelings with wry amusement; she would have been the first to acknowledge, indeed to claim, that no binding tie existed between herself and this in many ways unsatisfactory con man she had taken up with; certainly if some other man began to interest her there was no emotional bond with Bernard Arthur Daley which would be allowed to stand in her way; yet, for all that, behind the contemptuous 'I-couldn't-care-less' attitude with which she was presently going to dismiss the affair she was undeniably aware of a slight pique. She, a woman, didn't care for it that there should be another woman there. It annoyed her that Bunny should have felt the need for another woman; it surprised her slightly that he had possessed the initiative to get himself one. She didn't propose to make things easy for him.

'You're not usually in your dressing-gown at this time in the morning,' she said. 'Are you all right?'

'If you had phoned me yesterday to say you were coming up I'd have been expecting you.'

'Of course you would; but I've told you, yesterday evening I was out at the local pub.'

'I don't suppose you went there alone.'

'As it happens, I did.'

'Actually if you had rung you might not have got me. I was out yesterday evening, too.'

'A party?'

'Drinking.'

'Enjoyable?'

'You know how these things go.'

'Anybody interesting there?'

'There's always somebody one pals up with if it's only for conversation.'

'*Was* it only for conversation?'

'What the heck is this? Are you trying to grill me or something?'

'Don't get worked up, Bunny. I thought you would be glad to see me and hear how things are going.'

'Of course I want to hear how things are going. Christ, look at the money I'm laying out.'

'That's exactly what I've come to talk about – money. But we don't want anyone else in on that sort of conversation, do we?'

Bernard Daley did his best to look righteously indignant. 'What do you mean – "anyone else"?' he blustered.

'Come on, Bunny; stop acting like a naughty little schoolboy, which is all you are most of the time. She's in the bedroom, isn't she?'

'I never said there wasn't anybody there.'

'Well, for your information I regard that as my bedroom, so get her out of it, will you?'

At this point the bedroom door was flung open and a slightly built, red-headed girl flounced angrily across the living-room. She walked badly, tittuping on grotesquely high heels, and she was very cross.

'You told me you were all on your own!' she almost shouted at Bunny. 'Why the hell couldn't you say you had another woman knocking about the place?'

Bunny made a placatory gesture with his hands. Had he known what to say no doubt he would have said it. Dolly looked on in amusement, and the sight of her made the redhead angrier still.

'You weren't much use to me last night,' she told Bunny bitterly, 'and you're no bloody good at all now.' She strode out of the flat, and the front door slammed behind her.

'I'd like to wring her stupid little neck,' Bunny said, and the woman listening to him was surprised by the edge of viciousness in his voice. It occurred to her for the first time that the word ineffectual' which she often enough applied to him might not always be appropriate; he sounded as though he might be capable of turning really nasty. She was too sure of herself to take any alarm from the thought, but still it alerted her and, in a way, even amused her. 'That's a cheap little tart,' she taunted him. 'You ought to do better for yourself than that, Bunny.'

'Suppose we leave her out of it?'

'Gladly. It wasn't I who brought her in, I might remind you.'

'All right, all right. I brought her back here last night; she spent the night here; now she's gone; you saw her go; now for Christ's sake let's forget about the silly little bitch and talk about something that matters.'

'I'll get myself a cup of coffee,' Dolly said, 'if that woman hasn't messed up all the cooking arrangements.'

'She didn't touch the cooking arrangements,' Bunny almost shouted. 'She came back here, she's gone, she's finished. Can't you get that into your head?'

Dolly went to the so-called 'kitchen', which in reality was hardly more than a curtained-off corner of the living-room, and made herself a cup of Nescafé. She brought it back into the room and sat down opposite Bunny; she was so enjoying teasing him about his cheap little redhead that she was tempted to go on with it, but she thought it better to give the subject a rest and talk about their own affairs.

'How are things down at Farnbridge?' Bunny asked.

'I'm quids in.'

'You've got on friendly terms with him?'

'Very friendly.'

'What sort of chap is he? How old?'

'Twelve years ago he told me he was just eighteen, so that makes thirty, doesn't it?'

'You're not getting all starry-eyed over that first time you met him twelve years back, are you?'

'I finished being starry-eyed about things a long time ago.'

'I wonder. Some women never quite finish with it. What's he like? Tell me about him.'

The woman took her time over lighting a cigarette and

blew out a long, thoughtful plume of smoke before answering. Bunny watched her curiously.

'He's got a quick temper,' she said at last. 'He's quite capable of exploding suddenly about nothing at all. It doesn't mean anything. He's really quite a kid in some ways.'

'Is he getting fond of you?'

Dolly laughed. 'I think he's scared of women.'

'Is he a homo?'

'I haven't asked him.'

'Don't be silly. You can tell.'

'There's a man living with him at the Hall.'

'There is? Well, there you are, then; most likely he *is* a homo.'

Dolly smiled and shook her head. 'This man living there isn't a queer. He's a husky, conceited extrovert. They ought to do a double-page spread of him in the nude for *Playgirl*. I should think he would love that.'

'You don't sound as though you like him.'

Dolly flicked the ash off her cigarette and said, 'Like him? I don't give a damn about him one way or the other. To hell with him. Anyway, he's only going to be there for a short time to scare off the Press.'

'Are there any press people about?'

'No, none. They've lost interest.'

'A pity Pentallan isn't a homo; you might get some photographs.'

'Blackmail, you mean?'

'Blackmail? No, come off it, Dolly, who's talking about blackmail? But, all the same, if you were able to get some really compromising snaps it's quite possible, when you gave him a chance to think it over, that Pentallan wouldn't want a newspaper to get hold of them, isn't it? You don't threaten him in any way, of course; but if he wants to buy up the negatives you are quite willing to sell them, aren't you?'

The woman shook her head decisively. 'No, I'm not. Good God, Bunny, what's come over you? That *is* blackmail. Wrap it up how you like but that's what it is. I know it's blackmail, you know it's blackmail, the god-damned judge and jury will know it's blackmail. That's not our line at all. And in any case I don't like it. I wouldn't do it to Charlie.'

Bunny looked at her speculatively without speaking for a few seconds, and she continued, 'Charlie Pentallan has come into a lot of money. More than he needs. Maybe it wouldn't hurt him to lose some of it. O.K., that's one thing; but I'm not going to have any part in blackmailing him.

'All right. It was just an idea. Actually I'm inclined to agree with you. Too dangerous probably. And anyway it seems you don't want to hurt this Charlie of yours—'

'I don't mind separating him from some of his money. That's the game you understand, Bunny, and there's nobody better at it than you.'

He was mollified by the compliment, and the woman was glad to observe the fact; she found herself disliking the man intensely, but for better or worse, and for the present at any rate, they were partners, and there was no sense in falling out with him.

'Tell me a bit more about this other man,' Bunny said. 'Will he be in the way?'

'I'll tell Charlie to get rid of him soon.'

'And will Charlie do what you tell him to?'

Dolly ignored the sarcastic tone of the question and answered in a level voice, 'I dare say I can persuade him.'

'Why hasn't he married, this Charlie of yours?'

'I've told you already, he's scared of women.'

'Is he scared of you? Look out you don't frighten him off.'

'I won't frighten him. He wants someone to advise him; someone to advise him about money. I've made him see that already.'

Bunny smiled; the talk was turning towards his own specialised field, and he felt happier for it.

'Well, you haven't wasted your time down there entirely, then. I'll give him plenty of advice how to invest his money.'

'Not yet, though; not immediately; take it easy. I'll let

you know when to come on the scene.'

Bunny crossed the room to the kitchen corner and made himself a second cup of coffee. He carried it back to the table and sat down again opposite the woman. 'Well, that's fair enough,' he said. 'You know I never want to spoil any job by rushing things; but don't you go and get fond of him in the meantime. No nonsense like that.'

'It's the meantime I'm talking about. I've got to live in the meantime.'

'Live? What's happened to that five hundred I gave you the other day?'

'Five weeks ago. And I had to pay three hundred of it down, rent in advance, to be sure of getting the cottage.'

'Well, even if you did, that still leaves two hundred.'

'What's two hundred pounds these days?'

'It's a hell of a lot of money, these days or any other days; hundred-quid notes don't grow on trees I can tell you.'

In the end he reluctantly agreed to let her have a hundred pounds more, but not before they had come close to having an out-and-out quarrel.

'It's like your stupid little bets,' she twitted him at one point. 'You're afraid to put anything decent on so you never win anything decent.'

The man had to go to the bank to get the money and when he came back with it and handed it over he said, 'That will carry you on till it's time for me to come down and get things going. I reckon you must be having a damned nice holiday down there in the country. Get the mug fond of you, of course, but don't get up to any funny tricks, will you?'

Dolly looked at him steadily for a moment; she was on the point of making a scathing reference to cheap little redheads but she decided it wasn't worth it, it didn't matter; she said nothing; she stretched out her hand, took the twenty five-pound notes and stuffed them carelessly into her bag.

CHAPTER EIGHT

Dolly wasn't sorry to leave the mews or indeed London behind her; somewhat to her own surprise she felt a disenchantment for the place. When visualising her day she had planned a shopping expedition to Harrods, to Peter Jones and to a small hat-shop off Sloane Square. None of it worked out as she had hoped. Harrods had got just what she wanted, but not at a price she could afford; Peter Jones had sold out and had no idea when the next lot would be coming in; Sheila, who ran the highly individualistic hat-shop, was on holiday and Dolly didn't like the woman who was temporarily in charge.

She wasn't sorry, therefore, to get to Liverpool Street Station in time for the three o'clock train for Farnbridge. The train was already standing at the platform, and she was walking along it looking for an empty second-class compartment when a voice she hadn't heard for some six years hailed her from behind.

'Dolly Bennett – well, of all people!'

She swung round and there was Jimmy Loader, looking just the same as ever; but, on second thoughts, no, not just the same; a little more flushed in the face, a little more paunchy round the middle, but still very unmistakably the old Jimmy L.: fur collar; rakish hat; self-confidence oozing out of him.

'How I dislike this ghastly station,' he said. 'What are you doing here?'

'I'm catching this train, the three o'clock, to Farnbridge.'

'Farnbridge? Where's that? Never heard of it. What a bit of luck, though; I'm going on the three o'clock, too. To

Hertford. Here we are, here's an empty smoker.'

It was a first-class compartment, but Dolly didn't say anything. She wasn't going to admit to Jimmy Loader that she was travelling second. If an inspector came along she would have to pay the difference; she just hoped one wouldn't. Jimmy settled down in the seat opposite her, lit one of his long, thin cigars (Dolly remembered them well) and looked at her.

'Well, you're as handsome as ever, Doll,' he declared.

She laughed; she doubted if it was true; but still she didn't mind his saying it.

'And what on earth have you been doing with yourself all this time?' he went on.

She laughed again; she wondered what he would say if she told him about the last six years with Bunny. Not that Jimmy would have much right to be shocked, she thought; he was a bit of an old rascal himself in some ways.

'Oh, knocking about; you know – living.'

'Married?'

'No, I'm not married.'

'What the hell you left the profession for I'll never know.'

'You didn't get me enough jobs, Jimmy.'

'Aw, Doll, turn it up. You know how things go. You've got to soldier on. Nothing for six months, nine months, a year even; then suddenly, out of the blue, a plum – you find yourself in the West End for a twelve-month run.'

'I never did.'

'You weren't doing too badly. Plenty did worse, believe me.'

'I'm sorry for them, then; they must have had smaller appetites than me.'

'You don't look exactly starved to me, Doll. Get yourself back in *Spotlight* and the casting directors will say, "Who's this damned good-looking, mature woman here, play anything from twenty-five upwards?" What about those wonderful notices you had for your Mrs Mayfield in *Paid in Full*?'

'Mrs Maybury actually.'

'Maybury, then; what's it matter what the name was? You

got good notices for that, Doll. You got raves.'

'You can't eat rave notices. How have you been doing, Jimmy? You look pretty prosperous.'

'Prosperous? I don't know about that. I don't know what the word means exactly. Since last seeing you, Doll, I've been virtually broke twice, really wondering where next week's meals were coming from; and once at least I've been in the money, and somehow I've never stopped living pretty well.'

'Trust you to do that, Jimmy.'

'Well, dammit, we've all got to end up in our little boxes sooner or later, haven't we? We shan't be getting any joy then, so we may as well have fun whilst we can, that's my motto.'

'And what's happening in the theatre world? I haven't seen anything for, oh, I don't know how long – ages.'

'What's happening in the theatre? You may well ask.' Jimmy took a long pull at his cigar and studied the little cloud of blue smoke as he puffed it out into the compartment and it swirled and eddied in the moving air until it finally disappeared. 'Do you know, Dolly,' he went on, 'I was an idealist once. Still am a bit of a one for that matter. I know what people think about agents; they think once we've got our ten per cent that's all we care about. I know what they think about me – racing, gambling, living it up a bit. O.K., O.K., so I do live it up a bit; that doesn't prevent me from caring about acting. I'm mad about good acting; always have been; always will be, I guess. I can still come out from a play in tears. Jimmy Loader in tears! Anyone who sees me probably thinks it's because I'm pissed; but it isn't; it's because I've seen a piece of good acting. And what's happening in the theatre today is that there's hardly any real acting left. They've all gone mad to get into these commercials. The Dames and the Lords and all the rest of the people the profession is cluttered up with, they don't want to do Hamlet or Macbeth or Portia or Juliet anymore, they want a couple of minutes on the box advertising Doggomix or Katty-Curry. "For God's sake get me a commercial," screaming at me all the time. "That's where the easy money is." I tell you acting is dying out, at the top of the profession anyway. I fix them up with a commercial if I can and sometimes I switch the box on and watch them. I watch a man I know to be a really good actor, an artist, putting on a sickly smile and a treacly voice saying, "Chew chews are simply wonderful – try one." That's his artistic contribution to the evening and he'll pick up as much for doing that as he would for giving a carefully rehearsed, first-rate performance of the lead in *The Cherry Orchard*. And the silly sod is pleased about it. Less work, more money. That's what the commercials are doing to the top of the profession these days. Mind you, I say the top. There's still plenty of talent milling about lower down.'

'And, if I came back into the profession, what could you do for me, Jimmy?'

Jimmy Loader made a wry grimace. 'You've been out six years, Doll, haven't you? And things have changed. By God, I'll say they've changed. I wonder I'm not grey-haired with the worries I've been through. Still, I don't say they've changed for the bad altogether. Not altogether. Musicals are the thing now. In the last five years there have been some damned good musicals. And some disasters. My belief is there'll always be a public for a good musical. Good lyrics, good tunes and, if you can get it, a bit of a gimmicky idea to start with – it's a winning formula, I don't care what anybody says.' Jimmy drew once more on his cigar and then took it from his lips to add the pregnant words 'At least I hope it is.'

After her unsatisfactory day in London Dolly was thoroughly enjoying Jimmy's talk about the theatre; even if she didn't seriously entertain the idea of trying to get back into the profession, she was willing to listen to Jimmy's chatter about it for as long as he liked to go on, so now she prompted him with, 'Why, have you got a musical in mind, Jimmy?'

Jimmy's eyes had been studying the compartment roof; he now lowered them and fixed Dolly with the steady, almost vacant stare of someone whose thoughts are running far afield.

At length and with an emphatic nod he answered her question.

'Yes, I have. Don't bother to tell me it's silly. I know it's silly. Half the things I do in life are silly, and the other half are daft anyway, so what's the difference. I know the odds are all against it; but, there you are, sometimes you pull it off; sometimes the miracle happens. Remember Blue Border?'

Dolly shook her head. 'Blue Border? No. What was it? A play?'

'No, no. A play? For God's sake. Blue Border was a horse. One year it was pulling a plough – this horse actually was pulling a plough on a smallholding somewhere in Ireland – next autumn it had been bought by some sportsman and was being hunted; two years after that somebody else snapped it up, brought it over to this country and ran it up at Aintree in the National. It started an absolute outsider, sixty-six to one; it jumped like a stag all the way round and came in first by ten lengths Very nice, too, for anyone who had a hundred smackers on it.'

'Did you, Jimmy?'

'No, of course I didn't. I'm not around when luck like that is being dished out. But it taught me one thing; like I just said, sometimes the miracle does happen; you can find nuggets in the most unlikely places. Like these two chaps who have signed up with me. One of them is a marker in a billiards room; imagine that – a marker in a billiards saloon and a genius. That boy composes tunes like nobody's business. Music comes out of his ears; he thinks about nothing else. Set him down at a piano and put enough drink beside him and he'll play for ever. As far as I can make out he must know every goddam tune in the world and when he runs out of what he knows he makes up something of his own. And every now and again something that he makes up is good, and I mean good, really good, the sort of thing that sends 'em out of the theatre at the end of a show humming and whistling, a winner.

'He's got an off-sider, a boy friend, who writes the lyrics for him and hates doing it. Hates it. Lyrics are a waste of time, according to him; what he wants to get on with is a bloody great long novel. Half a million words it's going to run out to, and he says the publishers will be falling over themselves to get it. Well, under pressure I've read a few chunks of it in typescript and the only thing I can see happening is publishers falling over asleep with boredom. If that boy's a novelist I'm a world-class tennis-player. But get him away from this boring book of his, get him on to writing lyrics and he's brilliant; he's in the Coward and Cole Porter class.'

'And these two are writing a musical for you, Jimmy?'

'They've got this idea – I don't know which of them got it first, but it's a winner – of turning Sherlock Holmes into a musical. Making a sort of portmanteau of half a dozen of the best-known stories, sending it up a bit here and there and putting in a touch of love interest. Can't you see it all? Fog in Baker Street and the hansoms trotting by and the newspaper boys calling the evening headlines – it's got it all, nostalgia and excitement and romance; and you ought to hear some of the numbers we've got already – "Baker Street Blues" and "The Speckled Bandeau" – I tell you these two boys just don't know how good it is. But I do. When you've been in the game as long as I have you get a feeling. And my feeling is if we can get this thing started, give it a chance, we've got a gold-mine.'

'And when are you going to open with it?'

'Oh, my God, Dolly, open! Talk sense. We're nowhere near opening. It's all going to be pulled apart and put together differently half a dozen times yet. We've got casting, dresses, scenery, the score, a title, everything to think of yet. But that's how these things go. That's how a musical gets made. Open? By the time we come to talk about the opening date I shall be grey-haired, I can see that. And we shan't open at all unless I can get some more finance, some more money. Everyone says there's a lot of money about, but you try to get hold of any and it's a different story. I've got quite a lot of backing but I must have some more, and anyone who can be persuaded to back this idea is on to a gold-mine, I can tell you that. A gold-mine. You don't happen to know some nice old sugar-daddy who wants to turn, say, twenty thousand quid into something really big, do you?'

Dolly took her time before answering, and in any case Jimmy Loader was not expecting an answer; he was all the more surprised, therefore, when at last one came.

'I don't know about "old sugar-daddy" and I don't know about twenty thousand; but I think there is somebody who might possibly be interested, yes.'

Jimmy Loader lowered the window a few inches and threw out the butt of his cigar. He selected and lit another smoke, eyeing Dolly with speculative glances the while. Finally he said, 'You really know somebody who might be interested in the idea?'

Dolly nodded. 'Yes. It's a possibility.'

'I tell you this, Doll. You get somebody to put up the money for this show and I'll see there's a part written into it for you.'

'I can't sing, Jimmy.'

'You won't have to. They're not all singing parts. I'll see there's a nice, fair-sized part tailor-made for you – if you get the money. There won't be any parts for anybody, there won't be a show at all, unless we can find another backer. Are you telling me you've got yourself a nice soft billet with somebody who's loaded?'

'I'm friendly, getting friendly, with someone, a man, who has come in for quite a lot of money, yes.'

Jimmy smiled appreciatively.

'Trust you, Dolly, to land on your feet. I always did say you were a clever girl.'

The train began to slow down for Farnbridge, and gathering her bag and her evening paper together Dolly said, 'I'll see what I can do. I'm not saying more.'

Jimmy laid a finger on her forearm. 'You do that,' he urged.

'You see what you can do. And don't forget, if you can talk your boy friend into backing this show you'll be doing him a real good turn, you'll be putting him on to a gold-mine.'

'I'll see what I can do,' Dolly promised again.

The train came to a halt, and as Dolly got out Jimmy Loader's final admonition was 'And let me know as soon as you can, Dolly. The old place. Shaftesbury Avenue. The same old rickety stairs, and I might even have those done up if we get Sherlock Holmes off the ground.'

The chance meeting with Jimmy Loader in the train had a strong effect on Dolly; her thoughts kept returning to it for days afterwards. For half an hour she had felt in touch again with the world to which she had once belonged, a world which never wholly loses its hold over people who have once been addicts.

She thought Jimmy Loader could well be right about musicals; musicals probably *were* the thing now; after all, Jimmy was no fool; he had been tossed about in the stormy seas of theatrical agency for years and he was still afloat, still buoyant; still looking pink and prosperous and smoking cigars; every now and again the Jimmy Loaders of life, having backed losers and semi-losers for a long time, came up with a winner. Dolly had seen it happen before and she had a hunch that now it might be going to happen again.

If it *did* happen, and if she *did* manage to get in on the act, well it would prove that Bernard Daley was not the only person who could think up a profitable scheme; and the beauty of this scheme, she told herself, was that it wouldn't do anybody any harm; if Jimmy Loader was right and she felt in her bones that he could be – everyone concerned was going to make a packet. As for Jimmy's promise of having a part written in especially for her, she was at once excited and scared by the idea; sometimes more scared than excited, sometimes the other way round. Although thoughts about this project had been milling about in her head almost continuously since the meeting in the train, Dolly realised that she was not going to find it easy to broach the matter to Charlie Pentallan.

Why shouldn't I? she thought. After all, it isn't going to hurt him. And that thought brought, as it were, a curious shadow with it. What had been the whole point of establishing herself in Gorse Cottage? Hadn't hurting Charlie Pentallan been the sole object of the exercise?

Dolly's belief in what Madame Vana had taught her to regard as the pattern of things was reinforced one afternoon about ten days after the meeting with Jimmy Loader. Charlie Pentallan dropped into Gorse Cottage as he frequently did these days; whilst Dolly was setting out things on the tea tray he stood by the window idly looking at the *Daily Telegraph* which he had picked up.

'What a fuss they are making about *Purple Evening*,' he said.

Cup and saucer still in hand, Dolly looked up sharply. *Purple Evening* was the extravagant musical which after a year of triumph on Broadway was about to open in London.

Dolly had scarcely ever heard Charlie mention the theatre before, and that he should do so now, when her own mind was so full of the subject, seemed to her extraordinary – yet, perhaps, not so extraordinary when one remembered Madame Vana.

'The new musical?' she said.

'Yes, the show that's coming over from the States. The first night is going to be next week.'

'At the Shaftesbury.'

'It's going to be quite an occasion apparently. Some of the Royals are going to be there and everybody who is anybody.'

'Have you ever been to a first night, Charlie?'

'To a first night? No, I don't know that I have. It must be rather fun.'

'It's marvellous.'

'Why don't we go to this one?'

Dolly stared at him in silence for a moment.

'Why don't you and I go to this one?' Charlie repeated,

but looking at the *Telegraph* again he went on, 'Only I don't suppose we should ever get tickets now; it says here that the whole thing is sold out twice over already.'

'Would you really like to go, Charlie?'

'I'd like to take you to it, Dolly; I'd like that very much.'

'I might be able to get seats.'

'Could you possibly?'

'I can try.'

'Only two. Hooky Hefferman doesn't have to be in on this.'

'Of course he doesn't, Charlie. Just you and me.'

'Do try, Dolly. You would like it, wouldn't you?'

'I should love it, Charlie; absolutely love it. Anything to do with the theatre fascinates me. I believe you could get interested in it, too, you know; you're just the type.'

'Put me through to Mr Loader,' Dolly said to the bored female voice at the other end. When he came on the line, Jimmy himself didn't sound bored; he sounded rushed for time, excitable and irritable, his usual mid-morning state of mind.

'Who's this?' he demanded. 'Yes, yes, Jimmy Loader here. What is it? Who's speaking?'

'Dolly, Jimmy. Dolly Bennett.'

'Dolly—? Oh, *Dolly Bennett*. What do you want, Doll?'

'I want two seats for Thursday week.'

'Thursday week?'

'The first night of *Purple Evening*.'

'Jesus, Doll. What are you on about? *Purple Evening*? People are practically committing murder to get seats. This is going to be the first night of the year, girl.'

'I still want two seats, Jimmy.'

'Look, Doll, I'm busy. Old pals and all that, fair enough; but some other time, some other show.'

'Don't ring off, Jimmy. Listen, the man who can put up twenty thousand pounds for your Sherlock Holmes musical wants to take me to the first night of *Purple Evening*, and I've told him I can get two seats.'

'My God, you're crucifying me.'

'Two seats, Jimmy; two good stalls.'

'And the Crown Jewels as well, I suppose. What's your telephone number down there?'

CHAPTER NINE

Hooky watched the development of the affair between Charlie Pentallan and the woman in Gorse Cottage with amused and even sympathetic interest. If, indeed, it was an affair; with Charlie Pentallan it was very difficult to tell, and Hooky was by no means certain how far his employer's education in such matters had progressed.

Once, in El Vino, Hooky had heard Boozey French give a piece of admirable advice to an undecided dabbler in the intricate game of love. Boozey, propping up the bar in his favourite corner, had uttered his dictum: 'What you want, my young friend, is a large, fat, experienced woman.' The quip had amused Hooky when he had first heard it and he still regarded it as a sound general principle; whether it applied exactly in the current situation he was not sure. Dolly was not particularly large; she was certainly not fat; but she was undoubtedly experienced. On the whole Hooky was inclined to think that she would do Charlie good, unless.... The qualifying clause which hovered uncertainly (irrationally?) at the back of his mind was 'unless she is there for the express purpose of doing him harm'. There were times when it seemed an absurd idea; times when it did not seem so absurd.

Occasionally, when he got into bed Hooky found himself unable to sleep; on those nights, and if he had no professional problem to mull over, he had been wont of old to do his best to while away the blank hours by recalling interesting bridge-hands he had held; but now, at Pentallan Hall, he did have a professional problem on his hands, the problem of looking after Charlie Pentallan, and he was hardening in his opinion that Charlie was a young innocent, singularly unfitted to look after himself.

So, staring up at the darkened ceiling, Hooky didn't bother himself about triumphs and tragedies of the bridge table; instead he was more likely to hark back reflectively to the time when his professional instincts had been alerted and he had heard, if only faintly, warning bells ring.

'I've taken the tenancy of a cottage in Long Wood Lane from an old friend of mine, Colonel Fellows,' she had said at that very first encounter in Pentallan Great Wood. Hooky recalled the words perfectly. No warning bells then; nothing could have sounded more straightforward and simple. But Hooky also remembered perfectly what had been said in Gorse Cottage on the evening of the Seduction that Didn't Occur: *'So you didn't know Colonel Fellows before coming to Gorse Cottage?'*

'Never seen or heard of the man before in my life. It just all happened out of the blue.' Warning bell number one.

Warning bell number two rang when Hooky, as though looking at the rushes of a film, ran over in his head the scene in Pentallan Hall itself the first time that Dolly had come up for a drink.

'Perhaps you saw about it in the papers?'

'Collapsed in his club? No, I didn't see a thing about it. How frightfully sad for you.'

A very proper and kindly expression of sympathy, Hooky thought; but difficult to square with:

'Wasn't that a marvellous remark the hall porter at the club made when Charlie's uncle fell down in a fit? What was it? "It's not the sort of thing we like to happen at the club." Something like that, wasn't it?'

'I don't suppose he really said it.'

'It said in the paper that he did. I read it myself' – which was her later version.

It was these doubts about the lady calling herself Mrs Acton which persuaded Hooky to stay on at Pentallan Hall. It was true that he was picking up quite a useful salary for being there, and although Hooky had never considered the making of money to be the most important thing in life he had to confess that he had not yet learnt how to do without the stuff; but, in spite of a sizeable cheque each week, life in the country was beginning to pall a little. Hooky found himself missing the rag-bag and rough and tumble of London; the *far niente* business was considerably less *dolce* than it had been some weeks ago.

But the more he thought about Gorse Cottage the more he came to the conclusion that it might be his duty to stay for a while. It was possible, of course, to suggest a number of reasons why the present tenant should have taken on the lease – she was tired of living in London; she wanted to tuck herself away quietly in the country; and so on. Hooky could think up several reasons which she might well put forward and which indeed, at least by suggestion, she had put forward; the difficulty was he couldn't quite bring himself to believe any of them. One thing was absurdly clear: Boozey French's dictum about a woman scorned was being proved peculiarly apt. As quoted on the Dolly Acton index, Hooky Hefferman shares had taken a dramatic tumble; but the less she saw of him the more she managed to see of Charlie Pentallan, and Hooky was mightily exercised to know whether he ought to step in and warn his employer and if so at what point he should do it.

'Some people are coming tomorrow from the *County Illustrated* magazine,' Charlie told him one morning at breakfast, 'to take photographs of the house. Apparently they are doing a series of articles about different houses up and down the country. I'm not going to be here.'

'Wise man. Avoid the Press like the plague unless you want to land in all sorts of trouble.'

'So you'll deal with them, won't you, Hooky?'

'Leave 'em to me. I'll cope. Is there anything you don't want them to photograph?'

'No, nothing. No secrets.' Charlie smiled. 'Actually, I don't see much point in their coming; I like the house a lot, but there's nothing particularly historical about it. You can show them the maze, of course.'

'I'll lose them in the maze, don't worry. And you'll be away for the day, will you?'

'I'm going out for a picnic.'

'A picnic?'

'With Mrs Acton.'

'Oh dear, oh dear.'

'Why don't you say straight out that you don't like her?'

'Don't get het up, Charlie boy. And, anyway, it wouldn't be true. I do like Dolly Acton – in a way. I think she's a very attractive woman; but picnics with attractive women can be dangerous.'

'If you deal with the *County Illustrated*, I'll look after myself on my picnic.'

Hooky touched his forelock in a mock gesture of submission, although, indeed, it was not altogether mocking, since he was a great believer in the tune being called by the man who paid the piper.

'Just as you say, Squire,' he said. 'Leave the Press to me. Nothing to worry about.'

Next day the *County Illustrated* team arrived not at eleven o'clock as had been arranged but, infected by the pervading English disease of unpunctuality, all of forty-five minutes later. When the two of them climbed out of a small, unconvincing saloon car Hooky greeted them somewhat austerely.

'You're late.'

'Late? Are we?'

'You told Lord Pentallan eleven o'clock; it's now' – Hooky consulted his watch – 'exactly twelve minutes to twelve.'

The male part of the team laughed. 'Oh, that – well, we found it a bit hard to get organised this morning. Still, here we are. I'm Ray: I take the pics; and this is Mollie: she writes the stuff up. I take it you are not Lord Pentallan?'

'Lord Pentallan has had to go out on business for the day; but that's all right, I'll show you around.'

'Anything worth seeing?'

'Beauty,' Hooky pronounced sententiously, 'is in the eye of the beholder.'

The three of them made a preliminary tour to see, as Ray put it, 'if there was anything worth a picture'.

'Pretty dreary, old-fashioned dump' was his verdict.

Hooky had already taken a strong dislike to the long-haired know-all of twenty-three.

'Well, there you are, then,' he advised. 'You can use that as a caption. "Three splendid photographs of a dreary old-fashioned dump."'

'What, in the *County Illustrated*? Gosh, you don't know much about how the Press works, do you? Butter has to ooze out of these things. All hunky-dory and lovely. If I did what you're suggesting the Editor would eat me for breakfast; he'd castrate me.'

'Must be a sharp-eyed fellow, your editor,' Hooky said sourly.

Eventually photographs were taken of the drawing-room, and, upstairs, of Hooky's four-poster bed.

'Queen Elizabeth I slept in that bed,' Hooky announced.

The girl Mollie sharpened her pencil. 'Really?'

'Come off it,' Hooky laughed. 'Does anything in the house look even vaguely Elizabethan? The bed is probably a fine example of Maples 1909.'

'Has anyone interesting ever slept in it?'

'Only me.'

'I don't think I'll bother to mention that,' said Mollie.

Downstairs once more Ray was fascinated by the row of bells behind the green baize door leading to the servants' quarters. He read out the labels half to himself, half-aloud: 'The Blue Room, the Gun Room, the Admiral's Room, His Lordship's Room ... I suppose there was a bell pull in all these rooms and all you had to do was to give it a tug and someone came running to see what you wanted. Incredible, isn't it?'

'Quite incredible,' Hooky agreed. 'Nowadays you might be writhing in your death agonies. No good ringing any bells. You've got to ask your National Health merchant if he will be kind enough to see you. He finds he can just fit in an appointment in his surgery in four days' time and when he tells you it's vital for you to go into hospital at once you find you can't because all the hospital workers have withdrawn their labour so there's nobody on hand to withdraw your bursting appendix. There's progress for you.'

'You sound to me like a real reactionary,' Ray said. 'Surely you belong to a union of some sort?'

'Indeed, I do,' Hooky assured him. 'I'm a life member of the F.C.S.S.M.G.B.O.W.'

The young photographer repeated the initials enquiringly.

'The for-Christ's-sake-stop-moaning-and-get-on-with-a-bit-of-work union,' Hooky explained.

Outside one exterior shot of the house was taken and one shot of the celebrated maze.

'I remember we had something about the maze once before in *County Illustrated*,' Ray said, 'but nobody really seems to know the history of it.'

Hooky didn't know the history of the maze. 'I don't suppose it's got a history,' he said. 'It's an Edwardian folly. A bit of fun. Well designed, well made. It does its job splendidly. They tell me it's quite easy to get lost in it so that you never find your way out. Why don't you two try it?'

When the *County Illustrated* team had left, Hooky went to the butler's pantry to report the welcome fact.

'All clear, Skipton,' he announced. 'Enemy forces retreating in disorder.'

'The people from the Press have gone, have they, Mr Hefferman?'

'Vanished into thin air.'

Skipton gave the silver candlestick in his hand an extra polish. 'When I was footman at my last place before coming here, Mr Hefferman, that lot would have had to come round to the side door and lucky to be let in there, I can tell you.'

'Times have degenerated, Skipton,' Hooky said with feeling.

Charlie came back from his picnic rather earlier than he had been expected, and Hooky observed him with amused interest. He was obviously seething with suppressed excitement of some kind. *Post coitum* there should have been, according to the book, *tristitia*; there was no *tristitia* here, so presumably there had not been any *coitus*, which, all things considered, Hooky thought was probably a good thing. His employer was clearly fairly bursting with something to say, and Hooky, always an interested amateur of the human scene, was intrigued to know what it might be. Charlie's opening words on the subject surprised him.

'I expect you know something about the theatre, Hooky, don't you?'

'The theatre?'

'Mrs Acton, Dolly, was in the theatre, you know.'

'Was she, indeed?'

'In a repertory company. She doesn't act now, but she still keeps in touch.'

'And you've been having a lovely long talk about all her past triumphs?'

'It wasn't like that at all. As I say, she is still very much in touch with theatrical things, and this friend of hers is putting on a musical.'

Realisation began to dawn at the back of Hooky's mind. Like a lamb to the slaughter, he thought; but he didn't say it. He stared at his employer with the same sort of detached, yet horrified, interest with which a man might watch a fly blindly approaching the lethal web.

'A musical?' he prompted.

'Actually, it's a marvellous idea. Sherlock Holmes. A sort of potpourri of all the stories mixed up. Baker Street and hansoms trotting in the fog and, oh, you know, everything like that. Don't you think it's a good idea?'

'Could be,' Hooky admitted cautiously: actually, it had long been his conviction that dolled up with good enough tunes and lyrics almost anything could be turned into a musical; a musical on the Book of Job could be a hilarious winner given the right treatment. His reflections along these lines were interrupted by Charlie's next words.

'And Dolly thinks there might be a chance for me.'

'I had no idea you had ambitions about the stage, Charlie.'

Pentallan gave his high-pitched, nervous laugh. 'Good heavens, no. Me act? I wouldn't know how to begin. I'd die of fright. Nothing to do with going on the stage, of course not. Really, Hooky, sometimes you do say some frightfully stupid things.'

'Sorry to be such a dolt. Just tell me quietly in words of one syllable what it's all about and I'll do my best to understand.'

'Dolly thinks that if she puts in a good word for me this friend of hers who is getting up the Sherlock Holmes musical might be persuaded to let me put some money into it.'

Now realisation ceased to be a doubtful dawning at the back of Hooky's mind and became a clear, cold certainty in the forefront of his consciousness; and now, indeed, he uttered his thought aloud.

'Like a lamb to the slaughter,' he said.

'What on earth are you talking about?' Charlie demanded, and there was incipient anger in his voice.

'How much money are you going to be allowed to prop this thing up with?' Hooky asked.

'Dolly thinks she might be able to persuade this friend of hers to let me put in twenty thousand pounds.'

'The golden fleece,' Hooky said. 'And if Mrs Patrick Campbell Dolly Acton goes down on her bended knees and actually manages to persuade this theatrical chum of hers to take twenty thousand quid of your money what do you suppose you are going to get out of it?'

'Dolly says we shall all make a fortune.'

'How astonishing she should say that!'

'You obviously don't know anything about musicals, Hooky; but Dolly does. She knows it all. Look at some of the other musicals based on books, things like *Half a Sixpence* and *Oliver*. They made pots and pots of money for everybody connected with them, didn't they?'

'They probably did,' Hooky had to admit.

'So why shouldn't Sherlock Holmes?'

'It possibly might.'

'So why are you so damned superior and sarcastic about the whole idea, crabbing it all the time?'

'Keep your hair on, Charlie; I'm just advising caution, that's all.'

Charlie Pentallan gave no sign of intending to keep his hair on; he was quickly working himself up into one of his childish tantrums. 'I wouldn't have thought that caution had been the guiding principle of your life,' he said.

Hooky laughed a trifle ruefully at that. *'Touché,'* he said, 'but for God's sake think a bit before you do anything. Twenty thousand quid is a lot of money. And, believe me, one of the quickest ways of getting rid of money is to start backing theatrical shows. Half the time you'd do better just to get armfuls of five-pound notes and keep heaping them up on the bonfire – that way you get rid of the stuff just the same and you don't have any worries doing it. What I'm saying, Charlie, is don't start feeling for your cheque book before you've found out quite a lot. Who exactly is this mysterious friend of Dolly Acton's who, if he's in a good mood, might just be persuaded to let you give him twenty thousand pounds?'

'Don't be ridiculous. Who said anything about giving? I shall be *investing* the money.'

'O.K., you'll be investing it. On whose advice? How much do you really know about Mrs Acton?'

'I suppose you have worked up some ridiculous prejudice against Dolly now.'

'All I'm asking you is how much do you really know about her?'

'I'll tell you what I know about Mrs Acton, Hefferman,' Lord Pentallan said, speaking with unusual dignity. 'I know that I have never had many friends in life and she is turning out to be a very good one to me; and I know, too, that I am becoming very fond of her.'

Hooky recognised the sincerity of the words and was not a little dismayed by it; he could well imagine that Charlie Pentallan, suddenly caught up in the throes of a delayed attack of calf love, would be capable of all sorts of idiocies. He thought his next question would land him in trouble, but nevertheless it had to be asked.

'Has it never struck you as a bit funny that having met you in the past – all that pub-by-the-river business at Maidenhead – Dolly Acton should turn up out of the blue again and get herself the lease of a cottage almost next door to Pentallan Hall very soon after you came into the title?'

Charlie's face went white with anger.

'How dare you make such a suggestion?' he demanded.

'Charlie, I'm not making any suggestions—'

'You are. Of course you are. You are asking a question which suggests something beastly and dishonourable against a lady, and it's caddish of you.'

'Hold your horses, little man,' Hooky advised him, 'and don't start using silly words or we shall be falling out in a big way. I'm saying are you sure that Mrs Acton had not read about your uncle's death before she decided to take the lease of Gorse Cottage?'

'Yes, I am sure,' Charlie answered triumphantly, 'because she said so, definitely.'

'But people say such contradictory things, don't they?'

'And I suppose that now what you are suggesting is that Mrs Acton is a liar.'

'Charlie, grow up. We are all of us liars, at some time or other and about some things.'

'Why don't you say straight out, Hefferman, that you are jealous of me and Dolly Acton? She has told me how badly you behaved one evening when you escorted her back to Gorse Cottage from the village pub—'

'What an imagination that girl has got!'

'So why don't you come straight out with it and say you are jealous?'

'Because it wouldn't even begin to be true.'

'The fact that a thing isn't true would hardly stop you saying it according to your philosophy, would it?'

Hooky laughed. Life had long since taught him that everything has a beginning, a middle and an end; and he had become a past master at recognising ends. He recognised one now. Pentallan Hall had been an agreeable and lucrative interlude and now it was over. If he stayed on there would be a blazing row and Hooky, who at one time had found it hard to resist blazing rows, now found that he tended to avoid them if he could.

'Charlie,' he said, 'you're a nice enough chap in many ways but you are a bloody young fool.'

Childish anger suffused young Lord Pentallan's face.

'Please don't imagine that I am going to allow anyone in my employ to address me like that,' he said, which made Hooky laugh more than ever. He had always found pomposity amusing; when allied to indignant rage it generally became hilarious.

'Quite right, Charlie boy,' he said. 'Don't you stand for it. And you don't have to, anyway. I'm no longer in your employ as you put it. I resign, chuck my hand in; as from now, this minute, *ex hoc nunc*, if that means anything. In ten minutes flat I'll be packed and gone, and you can look after your silly little self. Watch out for the man-eaters.'

Skipton accompanied Hooky out to the waiting Jag. 'I'm sorry you are leaving, Mr Hefferman, really sorry.'

'Cheer up, Skippers,' Hooky advised him. 'There's a time for everything. Ripeness is all.'

Skipton smiled gravely. 'That may be, sir,' he answered, 'but in my opinion Lord Pentallan is going to miss you.'

'Mind where he looks for consolation,' Hooky advised cryptically as he let in the clutch and started down the long drive.

In the village he looked in at the Pentallan Arms to fortify himself for the journey and to bid good-bye to the landlord. Honest Tom Pacey was dismayed.

'Going, Mr Hefferman? Leaving? I got it in my head you were going to settle in the village, be one of us, like. And what shall I do for an opening bat now when the Thirty-second come down?'

'June the second. Don't worry Tom. It's in my little book. Hooky tapped his breast pocket. 'I'll be back for that; I won't let you down.'

'Mr Hefferman, I said it before and I'll say it again; you're a gentleman.'

'You will keep making these extravagant statements, Tom,' Hooky said, but he wasn't displeased.

CHAPTER TEN

Any regrets which Charlie felt at the disappearance of Hooky Hefferman from the Pentallan scene were swallowed up and more than compensated for by satisfaction over his own action in the matter. 'Please don't imagine that I am going to allow anyone in my employ to address me like that' was a very satisfactory sentence to have achieved. To have been brave enough to achieve. Charlie was well aware of his own essential cowardice, both physical and moral. He had a genius for sensing when matters of any sort were coming to a head and for managing to be absent when they did. A great shirker of issues was Charlie. He was all the more pleased with himself, therefore, for not having shirked the issue with Hooky. For having stood up to him. For having done something. 'Please don't imagine that I am going to allow....'

It had worked, too. Hooky had accepted it. Dammit, he had to accept it, Charlie flattered himself. I told him where he got off, and he got off.

Decisively managing his own affairs had never been a conspicuous part of Charles Manderville Fenton's life. He had been an only child, and a puppy needs others in the litter to pull it about, to harden it a little and to bring out a certain healthy aggressiveness in it. Charlie had had none of that. His mother, a small, wiry, nervy woman, might have been incapable of overlying him physically – she was hardly big enough – but spiritually, mentally and morally she had overlain her only child heavily and consistently. The *don'ts* and *bewares* and *take cares* fairly smothered the boy.

At his public school there had been a certain amount of bullying; nothing outrageous, nothing beyond what normal healthy young male animals growing up together might be expected to get up to. The masterful ones kicked and thumped a little; the submissive ones came in for the kicking and thumping. Charlie was always on the receiving end. After the fashion of boys' republics, if as he grew up he had shown himself good at games things would have evened out; a member of the school XV or the cricket XI needs no other accolade, he has won his status. But Charlie never had any success in games; he was physically afraid of rugger and he thought cricket boring and silly.

In his third year at school one of the prefects – a 'blood' in the language of the place – was attracted by the youngster's unsophistication and tried to seduce him. The attempt failed because Charlie was too scared to let himself follow any healthy natural instinct, especially if it involved intimacy with another human being; he was already a secretive and shut-in person, sometimes regretting that he couldn't reach out to others but more and more aware of the difficulty of doing it.

At Oxford he had naturally blossomed a little; but it had been only a very tentative and cautious blossoming; the riverside walk with Dolly on 'good old Jonah's' evening had been one of the highlights of it.

His mother's twin obsessions about security and possessiveness were satisfied when, as soon as he came down from the university, she secured a post in the City for him. It was reasonably well paid, in time it would be considerably better paid, and every day, after discharging his not very onerous duties, Charlie came home to his mother. Between Charlie's mother and her brother-in-law Percy Pentallan, who then held the title, there was never any communication. There had always been antagonism between the two Pentallan boys; and when the younger one, George, married, as his elder brother considered, far beneath him coolness hardened into complete indifference.

'We have nothing to do with the other branch of the family,' Charlie's mother used to say; and since Percy ('the other branch') might marry any day and produce an heir and in any case could be expected to live for another twenty years – the Pentallans were a long-lived lot – neither she nor Charlie gave any serious thought to the title coming his way. Charlie's mother died in middle age of cancer, and he had not fully recovered from the resulting sense of loneliness before Percy Pentallan collapsed in Farnel's and died on his way to hospital.

Within the space of twelve months Charlie had gained a title and a great deal of money and had lost what, grown man though he was, he still essentially needed: a mother figure to turn to.

He made a special journey to Gorse Cottage to give Dolly a report on the dismissal of Hooky; he was anxious to let her know the masterful way in which he had dealt with the matter.

'When I started to talk about the theatre he made a sarcastic remark about me going on the stage; of course, I told him I would never be the slightest good at it....'

Dolly was too astute to put in the conventional 'Oh, I'm sure you would'; instead she said, 'You can become involved in the theatre in lots of ways besides actually acting, Charlie; lots of interesting ways, and I'm sure you would enjoy that.'

'Yes, I know I would; but it was no use trying to get Hefferman to understand that. For one thing, he's too suspicious.'

'Suspicious?'

Charlie was almost too embarrassed to utter his next sentence, but finally he managed to get it out. 'He asked me how much I knew about you.'

Dolly moved to a side table and took a cigarette from a packet lying there. She lit it, drew in and expelled an addict's deep lungful of smoke before coming back to where Charlie stood, and asked, 'And how did you answer that, Charlie? How much *do* you know about me? What did you tell Hooky?'

'I told him that I'm the sort of chap who hasn't made many friends in life; I don't make them easily; and that I'm beginning to realise that you are just about the best friend I have ever had.'

The woman drew on her cigarette again, blew a plume of

smoke towards the ceiling, watched it dissipate into the air and then gave a short, hard, unhappy laugh.

'Oh, Charlie,' she said.

'Do you know what I think the truth is, Dolly?'

She looked at him in silence for a few seconds, the thoughts in her head running in unexpected and disturbing channels. Finally she laughed again and said, 'The truth? It's dangerous stuff is truth, Charlie. Tell me what you think the truth is.'

'I think Hefferman was jealous about me and you.'

Dolly nodded.

'Of course, I wasn't going to listen to his suggestions. I told him I didn't employ him for that.'

'Suggestions?'

Charlie didn't want to go into any greater detail about Hooky Hefferman's warning remarks and luckily for him he was saved literally by the bell – the telephone bell.

Dolly crossed to the instrument and picked up the receiver. She got very few calls at Gorse Cottage and she felt pretty certain who this would be. Her voice hardened perceptibly when she answered.

'... Yes.... No.... It's not convenient. I've got a visitor; call again.'

She replaced the receiver and explained with an apologetic laugh, 'Sorry about that. It's the electricity people. Something has gone wrong with the cooker, and they want to come out and look at it.'

In the past five years she had told a large number of lies without giving a thought to the matter; now she was astonished at the reluctance she felt about telling this one.

'If you have trouble cooking here you can always come up to the Hall for a meal; you know I should like that.'

'Oh, I shall be all right, Charlie. Not to worry. But that's kind of you all the same, and I will come up for a meal with you now and again.'

'Please do; as often as you like.'

'So what happened next with Hooky?'

'He forgot his manners and called me a bloody young

fool. I wasn't going to stand for that, of course, so I told him he could pack up and go. Just like that.'

'Good for you, Charlie.'

'In a way I didn't like doing it. I hate rows.'

'Of course you do.'

'And I liked Hooky. I liked having him around.'

'You're better off without him.'

'And anyway—' Charlie gave a little, half-embarrassed laugh before continuing, 'You know what I said a moment ago about Hefferman being jealous – well, it cuts both ways.'

'How do you mean, Charlie?'

'I'm glad he has gone because I didn't want him to get too fond of you; or you of him. There!'

Dolly reached out and for a moment laid a hand on one of Charlie's.

'I've seen too many men like Hooky in my life,' she said.

'I didn't want him to get in the way of you and me and this theatrical business, this musical.'

'I suppose he has told you not to put any money into it?'

'More or less, yes.'

Dolly considered for a moment before she replied; a lot of unusual feelings were assailing her, and the most surprising of them was a sense of relief at being able to make her next remarks with conviction and sincerity.

'Look, Charlie, anything to do with the theatre is a toss-up and I'm not going to pretend it isn't. There aren't any certainties one way or the other. Just take two examples – more than twenty years ago a very ordinary thriller was put on at the Ambassadors with no particular stars in the cast. The critics gave it very middling notices. All the experts said it would be lucky if it ran three months. It's still packing them in, more than twenty years later. Twenty years in the West End!

'Then, who would have thought, in this day and age that anyone dare risk putting money into a musical about the last few days in the life of Jesus Christ, with numbers about the Ten Commandments and the Beatitudes and all the rest of it?

I'll bet most of the possible backers who had the idea put up to them pretty well died laughing at it. But who's laughing now? You just can't tell. All I'm saying is that I quite honestly think Jimmy Loader is on to a good thing in this Sherlock thing has a beginning, a middle and an end; and he had Holmes idea. Jimmy is one of those characters who have got the theatre in their bones. God knows how he was educated – I shouldn't think he *was*, not in any way to count; and I can't imagine how he was brought up. I should think he must have been a call boy from the age of ten, if they have them that young. He couldn't write two lines of dialogue if he tried for a month, and as for acting he wouldn't know where to start; but for all that, as I say, he's got the theatre in his bones. He's got a nose for it. He'll be in it till he dies. He's had some ups and downs; but sooner or later, and just once in a lifetime, a man like Jimmy Loader is due for a big success. And this musical he wants you to back could be it.'

Charlie listened to all this with intense interest, and when he spoke he said something that took Dolly by surprise.

'Of course everybody thinks that I've got a lot of money.'

Somewhat taken aback, Dolly laughed and said, 'Count me among everybody, Charlie. Haven't you?'

'Well, there's a lot of money about, if you know what I mean; but it's not all that straightforward; it's tied up in all sorts of ways with property and trusts and entailments. Dammit, in the end I believe the lawyers and accountants will do better out of it than I will! But still I can manage twenty thousand all right; and I think it's absolutely marvellous of you, Dolly, to give me the chance.'

'I honestly think you won't regret it, Charlie; I do honestly think that. That's honest.'

Charlie smiled. 'I would never expect you to be anything other than honest,' he said.

It was entirely characteristic of Charlie Pentallan to be caught up in a new enthusiasm to the exclusion of almost everything else. Before Dolly's suggestion about backing the musical he had hardly given a thought to the theatre; now it seemed he hardly gave a thought to anything else. Now it was all theatre. The toy which had so amused him when he had first taken up residence in the Hall had suddenly lost all its charm. Now the macaws, the budgerigars, the tawlins and the little grey birds with yellow spots which had once made Hooky so impatient were all forgotten. Now it was hurrying over to Gorse Cottage to talk theatre with Dolly, or summoning her over to the Hall for the same purpose. Naturally the visit to the first night of *Purple Evening* fanned the flames of this new fire.

When Jimmy Loader rang up Dolly to tell her that two tickets were available he left her in no doubt about how lucky she was and how much in his debt.

'I've had to perjure myself and make a life-long enemy over this, Doll. I'm not sure even now how I did it. Don't tell me I can't work miracles. I'll be walking on water next. Just you take care to bring your sucker up to scratch.'

'Jimmy, he's not a sucker. Not this time; not in that way. He's a nice little guy.'

'Well, whatever he is, I shall want that twenty thou out of him.'

It was a long time since Dolly had been to a first night; Charlie had never been to one, and in his impressionable state he found it heady stuff. Dolly got him to Shaftesbury Avenue in very good time; the theatre foyer was alive with light and with the noisy and excited chatter of the regular firstnighters, celebrities theatrical and otherwise, who already packed it. Every moment more people were arriving, fresh greetings being called; more noise, more excitement. Clearly it was an occasion and an occasion with the unmistakable smell of success about it. It was one of those times when you felt certain the ship was going to have a triumphal voyage even before she was actually launched.

When the last of the rapturously enthusiastic calls had been taken and the curtain finally came down the scenes in the foyer were repeated in a minor way backstage. For once there was hardly any anxiety about what the critics would say; the only speculation was what terms of praise they would use.

Jimmy Loader didn't think much of the gentlemen who wrote dramatic criticism for the daily press but this time he didn't fear them. 'Even those sarcastic sods can't do a carve-up job on this lot,' was his opinion. 'They've got to like this one.'

Years ago Dolly had been in the same repertory company as one of the minor members of the *Purple Evening* cast and on the strength of this she had taken Charlie backstage after the show. He was intensely excited by it all and not a little bewildered; everybody seemed to know everybody else, and the air was thick with 'darlings' and 'wonderfuls', and in her star's dressing-room the leading lady was holding what was almost a royal court.

Outside there might be a thin, cold rain falling and the posters of the evening papers might be proclaiming every sort of horror and disaster; all that didn't seem to matter here, in this shut-away world feeding joyously on itself and on its own make-believe success.

Coming away from the lesser dressing-room which they had visited they met Jimmy Loader hurrying along the narrow, bare-walled passage, and it was then that he said his piece about his pet abomination, the dramatic critics.

'And, Jimmy, this is Lord Pentallan,' Dolly said with heavy emphasis.

Jimmy ran a shrewd eye over his twenty-thousand-pound prospect; *Dolly's got him sewn up all right* was his conclusion.

'Very nice to meet you, Lord Pentallan,' he said.

'Charlie's interested in the theatre, Jimmy.'

'We're always on the look-out for people with fresh ideas,' Jimmy said rather pompously, hoping that what he really meant ('with fresh capital') wouldn't be too obvious. 'You must bring your friend to see me one day soon, Dolly, and we'll have a talk, O.K.?'

'I'll do that, Jimmy.'

'No good here, now, with all this excitement and noise going on; but soon, mind you, in a day or so, eh?'

Dolly nodded.

'And, Dolly,' Jimmy was already moving away, 'don't forget.

If Sherlock Holmes gets off the ground there'll be a part in it for you.'

'O.K., Jimmy, O.K., O.K.'

The following day at Pentallan Hall Charlie could talk of nothing but the excitements of the first night and the thrill of going behind. The prospect of becoming part of the theatre world had gone intoxicatingly to his head, and he had become completely hooked on the idea.

'When shall we be going to see Jimmy Loader again?' he wanted to know.

'In a day or two. I'll get in touch with him. As soon as I can fix it with him.'

'Do you suppose the first night of Sherlock Holmes will be like yesterday?'

Dolly laughed. 'Let's hope so,' she said, 'but we're a long, long way off the first night yet, Charlie.'

'I suppose there must be an awful lot to do.'

'When a musical is being got together there are plenty of times when you think nothing can ever possibly come out of it; but still, as they say, that's show-business.'

'Show business – I certainly never thought I'd be in it. What did Jimmy Loader mean about a part for you in the musical?'

Dolly had been devoutly hoping that Jimmy Loader's parting remark, made as he was already moving away, had gone unheeded. But obviously it hadn't, and so now it had to be dealt with.

'Charlie, I was upset about that.'

'Upset? Why?'

'Just like Jimmy to blurt things out like that without any explanation or anything.'

'But why should you be upset?'

'Well, now you are almost certain to think that the reason I'm suggesting that you should back the show is because I'm going to get a part in it. And it isn't that at all.'

'I never thought it was.'

'Honestly it isn't, Charlie. If Jimmy offered me a small part

I suppose I would take it; in fact I *would* take it, but after being out for six years I'd be scared to death.'

'I bet you'd be marvellous, Dolly.'

'It isn't because I might get a part, Charlie; it's because I think Jimmy's on to a winner at last; and, if he is, everyone connected with the show will make money.'

'I keep telling you I think it's wonderful of you to give me the chance. It's marvellous luck for me that you happened to come to Gorse Cottage. And, actually, if I come to terms with Jimmy Loader and agree to put up the money – and I'm sure I shall – I shall make it a condition that he gives you a part in the show. It will be a sort of joint affair; you and me, Dolly; I'll be backing the show and you'll be acting in it. How's that?'

'Oh, Charlie, you're really rather a sweet person.'

CHAPTER ELEVEN

Hooky's disappointed gaze told him at once that Boozey was not in his usual place at the end of the bar, and as a result the whole place immediately lost something of its atmosphere; the High Priest being absent, the ritual was a little flat. Younger, lesser, drinkers were there doing their best, but they lacked the Master's touch. Hooky made enquiries behind the bar and was told: 'Mr French's compliments to his friends, sir, and if any of them want to stand him a drink he will be in the Marquis of Hereford in the King's Road; so if you wish to see him especially, sir, that's where you will have to go.'

Remembering his last visit there Hooky had no objection whatsoever to paying a return call on the Marquis and when he opened the door and stopped to enter the delightful Edwardian interior he saw her at once. As he remembered her: the stately Junoesque figure, the glossy hair piled high in fantastic coils, the disturbing cleavage. She smiled slowly when she saw him.

'I told you I'd be back,' Hooky said.

She inclined her head in acknowledgement and answered, 'Men don't always do what they say; but I thought you would.'

Boozey French was standing at the far end of the bar; in a pub he always chose one end of the bar and he always chose to stand. Bar stools in his opinion were for weaklings: 'There are only two sensible positions in a bar,' he was wont to say, 'flat on your feet or flat on your face.'

He greeted Hooky's arrival with such evident pleasure that Hooky felt touched.

'A stranger from civilised parts,' Boozey cried. 'What brings you here, Hooky?'

'The news that you had deserted El Vino.'

'Only for today; only for this occasion; only because the blasted Lord has sent me off on one of his crack-brained ideas, a *gamine* hunt. I'm in the chair, Hooky, and I desire to take wine with you. Do you know that at one of those dreary literary nosh-ups they actually use that formula? The poor fish who has been fool enough to let himself be talked into taking the chair for the evening gets up halfway through the proceedings and bleats out "Gentlemen" – they are writers really, Grub Street hacks, but he calls them "gentlemen"; by such illusions do men feed their minds – "gentlemen," he says, "I desire to take wine with you"; and they all raise their glasses of plonk and look very solemn and say what a wonderful thing tradition is— What the hell am I on about, Hooky?'

'God knows, but you're in good voice. Carry on.' Hooky had already observed a certain glassy-eyed appearance unusual in so hardened a performer as Boozey; but sober, or only half-sober, Boozey could be good company and his acerbities were always worth listening to.

'Are you going to have a Pimms?' the panther behind the bar enquired. 'I remember you did the last time you were in and I imagine you are a person of habit.'

'Of bad habits mostly,' Boozey put in, but Hooky felt flattered that the panther remembered him; he thanked her with a smile that did not go unanswered.

'And what have you been up to, Hooky?' Boozey asked.

'Leading the rural life.'

'No wonder you look depressed.'

'Ah, but I was busy. I went there on a job. And I was doing all right until I was dismissed.'

'I suppose her husband came back unexpectedly and found you at it, a flagrant derelict as they say.'

Hooky laughed. 'Not this time. In fact I actually resisted temptation. A foolish thing to do, I know, what with life being short and opportunities getting fewer; but we are all guilty of idiocy at times and resist I did. I got mixed up with the new Lord Pentallan and went with him to ward off the press boys.'

'Was anybody interested? I didn't see any follow-up to the business in Farnel's.'

'Peggy Shelton showed up.'

'My God, that woman!' Boozey said, adding thoughtfully in one of his occasional moments of poetic inspiration, 'I'd never want to meet, unless entirely pissed.... That frightful thing, a Female Columnist – a rough translation, by the way, of one of the Odes of Horace.'

'I'm afraid I've forgotten all my Greek,' Hooky said, 'but I got rid of Peggy all right; she presented no difficulty.'

'Were there any difficulties?'

'Difficulties? No. Dangers? I'm not so sure.'

'Danger. What sort of danger? Being chased by a bull across a field, you mean? I can't imagine you in the country, Hooky. Come to that, I can't imagine the country. What did they do all day? Make daisy chains? Morris dancing on the village-green, incest, and so on? What did *you* do all day? Don't tell me if it's anything boring.'

'For one thing I slept in a four-poster bed, which has always been one of my minor ambitions.'

'Shun ambition, Hooky. By that sin fell the angels. And, God knows, you're no angel. By the same token you haven't got far to fall, which incidentally is what I should almost certainly do at this moment if I abandoned the support of this admirable bar.'

'One of those mornings, is it, Boozey?'

'As you say, one of those mornings. Brother Body has unfortunately failed to stay the course but Brother Brain remains alert. Not only alert but clear-sighted, far-ranging and seething with imaginative energy. At this very moment, Hooky, I could sit down and write a masterpiece. The great novel of our generation. Packed with pathos, love, horror and humanity and all the other nonsense that the Great British Public has been told it wants. Bursting with bawdiness, too. It's all there, boiling up in my head.'

'I'd let it stay there, if I were you,' Hooky advised.

'What else happened in your rural retreat? Presumably you didn't stay in your four-poster bed all day? Unless of course something was in it with you. Even then you would have to get out occasionally for a cup of tea, one imagines. *Was* there an Amaryllis sporting in the shade?'

'Amaryllis was in a place called Gorse Cottage actually.'

'Sounds prickly; but I don't suppose that would deter you, hardened lecher that you are.'

'Actually, I didn't sport with her; I spurned her.'

'Wise man. The monstrous folly of fornication! What a condition for the Creator to bind on his world that we've all got to be at it all the time – worms, flies, dogs, humans, the lot; sweating, heaving, panting, jerking; writing poems about it, making it the plot of almost every book and play that was ever written, the nub of every joke. God dammit, Hooky, can't mankind ever think about anything else?'

'Well, I did occasionally think of other things in Gorse Cottage. I wondered what Amaryllis was doing there.'

'What did you think she was doing?'

'When a man suddenly comes into something over a million pounds all sorts of things are liable to happen. You begin to be suspicious.'

'What kind is the new Peer of the realm? What wonderful addition has been made to the ranks of our legislators? What bursts of brilliant silence may we now expect from the Upper Chamber?'

'I was beginning to like the little guy. Quite a lot. Of course he's a lightweight. He doesn't really know what the world is all about. His balls have hardly dropped yet. That's his danger. That's what makes him vulnerable. He's the kind of defenceless little twit who's always looking for a mother. And like all these little, essentially insecure chaps he suddenly thinks it's time to stand on his dignity – Christ knows, there isn't a great deal of it for him to stand on – and he flies off the handle into a chattering rage. Like he did when he gave me the sack.'

'You've been dismissed, Hooky?'

'Thrown out on my ear. I spoke out of turn to my employer. A bad thing to do when your employer has lately come in for a million. Having a million gives a man inflated ideas about himself. So it was probably time for me to go. Yet, I'm sorry in a way; I've an idea things might get interesting down there. What brings you to this part of the world, Boozey?'

'The latest whim of the Lord. The senile old sod gets visited with what he thinks are these brilliant ideas every now and again. When he does he picks up one of the five telephones – do you realise that in that hideous house of his in Hampstead that man has no fewer than five telephones by his bedside? All I want by my bedside is a bottle of Bell's whisky and Boswell's *Life of Johnson.* He picks up one of these five telephones and starts screaming down it and scaring everyone to death.'

'Are you frightened of him, Boozey?'

The ageing man with the rather puffy face, leaning heavily against the bar counter, pushed his glass forward and said to the panther, 'Replenish my glass, Diana of the Ephesians, and don't overdo the soda so that I may have the moral courage to tell my inquisitive friend here who asks such awkward questions that, yes, I am frightened. Of course, time was when I wasn't going to be frightened of anything. God dammit, I had Life licked then. I was rushing about on my white charger of ambition, waving my pen in the air and on fire with a host of furious fancies. That masterpiece of a novel I told you about a few minutes ago very nearly got written. In fact the only reason it didn't get written was that I was so certain I could do it. So no need to hurry.'

Boozey took a large, thoughtful gulp from his replenished glass. 'Or was that someone else, and in another world?' he went on. 'Must have been, must have been. But that's all shoved be'ind me, long ago and fur away – every now and again Rudyard K. comes up with a real winner. It goes, Hooky; it leaves you. The essential quiddity seeps out of you, drains away. You say too many smart things, lean up against too many bars. People expect to see you leaning there, saying the smart things. Dammit, you can't let your public down, can you? So you let yourself down instead. Or do you? I doubt it. I think it's all written down before you start. I think there are marks in the sand which tell you which way you've got to go. Free will? Free will, my arse. Free nothing. I get a laugh by telling people what a scabrous paper I'm on, but I know damn well that if any one of them could get my job by cutting my throat he would cheerfully cut it tomorrow, which is what is known as the camaraderie of Fleet Street, the glorious brotherhood of the Press. And I know damn well, too, that when the Lord is visited by one of his whims and gets on the blower to me and tells me to get on with it I touch my cap and do just that; I get on with it.'

'And what is the latest order from on high?'

'Sing the praises of youth. The salvation of the world – and in my opinion only a lunatic would want to save the bloody thing – lies with babes and sucklings. The young are to be sought out and cracked up.

> "You are old Father William," the young man said,
> "And your hair has gone perfectly white;
> And yet you continue to poke like a stoat.
> Do you think at your age it is right?"

Somebody must have quoted this at the Lord and he saw the force of it. So at the moment Youth is everything, and "Things I Hear about Town" has got to be full of it.'

Hooky looked enquiringly round the bar.

'Ah, I'll be meeting her any minute now,' Boozey explained. 'I'm taking her to lunch and she said not in that dreary old West End; isn't there some new little place down the King's Road everyone is talking about? Which just shows you how naïve a tough little sex-pot can be; anything resembling animation in the King's Road has been dead and embalmed these three years. Euclid must have had it in mind when he made that crack about something having length but no point. Still Kenny's has come into existence, and since she wants to go there and the Lord will be paying the bill that's where I propose to take her.'

'Who is this youthful charmer?'

'Alvita Domanez.'

Hooky looked blank and then shook his head. 'Doesn't ring any sort of bell with me,' he said. 'Never heard of her.'

'Nor has anybody else yet. The Lord proposes to change all that. His fiat has gone forth: "This one has got something, build her up." And to give the old Bible-punching fraud his due he's probably right about her having something. The Lord has always had an uncanny knack of spotting talent – witness the fact that he employs me.'

'We all have our aberrations at times,' Hooky pointed out. 'What did you say her name is – Domanez?'

'Alvita Domanez. Parentage unknown, but I'd make a guess at a Jewish-Austrian-German-French mixture possibly with a dash of Arab squeezed in. A camel driver for a father probably. Or even a camel. You can't say she's pretty, but by God she's full of life. Sex fairly oozes out of her. She's a classic example of the type that gets thrown up every now and again, the *gamine* brothel-born and slum-reared, the gutter genius.'

'Is she a genius?'

'Probably. The Lord says she has got to be cracked up as one anyway. And, Hooky, I'm too old to cope with youthful geniuses. Too old this morning anyway, and possibly a step too far advanced in my devotions to Bacchus. It happens sometimes. So give me a hand, Hooky, will you?'

It was the first time in an acquaintance now of several pretty hard-bitten years that Hooky had heard such an admission from the acknowledged High Priest of Serious and Sustained Drinking, and he was touched by it. Boozey looked ill and care-worn and listless. The poor old sod, Hooky thought in sudden sympathy. It's all empty for him; there's nothing there.

'Anything I can do for you, Boozey,' he said.

'Have lunch with us.'

'With you and the sex-pot?'

'It will help me if you do. These bloody budding geniuses expect one to sparkle all the time. The sparks have gone out of me, Hooky. For this morning at any rate. You can do the sparkling whilst I sober up; and I'll give you a nice para in my column tomorrow.'

'And where do we meet this camel driver's daughter?' Hooky enquired.

'At Kenny's.' Boozey glanced up at the clock. 'Now. Come on, we must be going. If we keep her waiting she'll probably start throwing things about. Let's hope she hasn't brought one of her father's camels with her.'

'Come again,' said the panther behind the bar, watching Hooky's departure with slumbrous eyes.

At Kenny's, when she finally arrived, she had not brought one of her father's camels, but otherwise she was very much as advertised and according to Boozey's schedule: dark; small; bursting with energy and life; the voice almost harsh; the eyes large and magnetic. Sex certainly oozed out of her, as Boozey had said it would, but so did brash and unsuppressible self-confidence. The world? Pooh, a fig for the world. The world could be conquered. The ladder of show-biz was there, she had managed to get her foot on it and by God she was going up it, right to the glittering top. After the first five minutes of knowing her Hooky felt that there and then he could have written her total biography, start to finish: she would be a furore; she would almost certainly be divorced three times and bankrupt at least twice; at the age of eighty (to which she wouldn't admit), with a raddled face and ill-fitting wig, she would still be capering about, still avid for publicity, still hungering for the grease-paint and the applause.

She was totally and devastatingly capable of looking after herself and she summed up the two men lunching with her at once: one over the hill, but by reason of his press connections still with power in the magic world of publicity, useful therefore and not to be neglected; the other tough and masculine, ready, at a guess, to respond to anything she cared to put out; but was he worth it? Did he matter? Could he help her?

Boozey, who had astonishing powers of recovery, was beginning to surface again at the end of the first five minutes and he gave his attention to what was for him the all-important part of the meal, the Canon of the Menu as it were.

'Shall I order the wine?' he suggested taking the imposing-looking wine-list in hand.

'Of course. A man ought to do that. I'm sure you know all about wine' (the wide, red mouth smiled flatteringly; the large, dark eyes were scornful; she didn't really think this one knew all about anything; she thought he was done, finished; halfway to Skid Row). 'But for me' – those remarkable hands, ugly yet compellingly powerful, made a dismissive gesture – 'nothing.'

'No wine?'

'Nothing. I don't drink.'

Hooky wasn't altogether surprised; the only drink this one wanted, he thought, was the wine of success. 'And what are you planning to do in the theatre, Miss Domanez?' he asked politely.

'I'm going straight into a new West End musical.'

'Good for you. You certainly haven't wasted any time, then.'

'I don't waste time. Why should I? What is there to wait for? I've got the talent; they want it. Why wait?'

'A new musical?' Boozey queried.

'For the West End. This morning I have been seeing this man called Loader. Jimmy Loader. You know Jimmy Loader?'

'Everybody knows Jimmy Loader. Man and boy he's been dodging about in things theatrical since time was.'

'You think he is good?'

'He's the sort of man you can't keep down. On the Day of

Judgement he'll be signing up the Archangel Gabriel for the exclusive rights on the record of his trumpet solo.'

'You think he will make good? Succeed?'

'Jimmy's the sort of chap who might easily come up with a winner one day.'

'This time he will. You've heard of someone called Holmes, Sherlock Holmes?'

'Sherlock Holmes? Everybody has heard of Sherlock Holmes.'

'Well, there you are, then. That is what Jimmy Loader says. So everybody will go to see the musical about Sherlock Holmes.'

'And you are going to be in it?'

'Jimmy Loader has promised me a part this morning.'

'What part?'

'God knows. I don't. I don't mind. The part doesn't matter. I'm *me*. It's me that matters. Jimmy knows that. He has seen me. He wants energy, fire, sex, *life* on the stage and he knows I can put them all there. Look' – she raised one hand in the air above the table, the strong fingers held upwards in the shape of a cup – 'I'll hold the audience *like that*; in my hand; I'll do what I want with them.'

Watching her, fascinated, Hooky thought that she very probably would, too.

'And when does this thing get off the ground?' Boozey asked.

'Soon. It's all boiling up. There's finance to worry about,' she shook her head, half in amusement it seemed, half in anger. 'Let Jimmy Loader worry about the money. I never do. Jimmy says he will get the rest of the money O.K.'

'I think he will,' Hooky chimed in. 'I think Jimmy will get his backing all right.'

'And what the hell do you know about it?' Boozey demanded.

'More than you might think.'

Boozey replenished his glass and raised it in a hand that miraculously hardly shook at all.

'Here's to all you cheerful optimists,' he said. 'God knows what you've got to be optimistic about, but good luck to you.'

CHAPTER TWELVE

It had become a habit lately for Dolly to walk over from Gorse Cottage in the middle of the morning for a glass of Madeira and a biscuit. The taciturn Skipton was beginning to relax the rather stiff manner he had been inclined to adopt at the outset towards his new master. Charlie Pentallan had that effect on all sorts of people, of making them feel that he needed to be looked after and that they were the people to do it. So every now and again, and often apparently apropos of nothing, Skipton would give out bits of information about the Hall and its domestic arrangements. 'His late Lordship was very fond of Madeira,' he told Charlie one day. 'Very fond indeed. A glass of Madeira and a biscuit at eleven o'clock was something he never missed. Never. Regular as anything he was about it. And, of course, I've plenty still left in the cellar.'

Charlie didn't fail to notice '*I*'ve plenty still left', not 'you' or even 'we'; but he made no comment; he was rather scared of Skipton.

'If there's plenty still left,' he said, 'I don't see why I shouldn't try it for elevenses; if it was good enough for my uncle it's good enough for me.'

Skipton smiled approvingly; he was a great believer in tradition. Accordingly the glass-of-Madeira-and-biscuit-at-eleven ritual was established, and right from the beginning Dolly was invited to share it. She discovered that she actually enjoyed the walk to the Hall: there was very little traffic in Long Wood Lane and none at all once she turned into the Trackway; here the hedges grew rampantly on either side and wild wayside flowers grew beneath them; her movement might startle a blackbird into angry protest at such an intrusion into his privacy and once just after taking the footpath into Pentallan Great Wood she saw a fox, the first she had ever seen, standing stock still not twenty yards away, black muzzle uplifted to test the tainted air, delicate ear pricked in readiness to catch the first sounds of danger.

Dolly stood as still as the fox, and for five long seconds they stared at one another; the woman and the animal; the creature who lived almost entirely at second hand and the creature who was still splendidly elemental, embedded deep in the life pattern. Almost as though it were saying, 'You're only a human; you are not as fleet of foot as I am; you can't decipher the smells and sounds of the woodland as I can; I can see that you haven't got with you any of the things that would make you dangerous to me – a gun, a stick, dogs – I have no fear of you whatsoever, in fact I despise you,' the fox dropped his incredibly sensitive muzzle and unhurriedly trotted off into the undergrowth about his business.

Dolly was entranced by the encounter and strangely affected by it. A live wild animal in the woods! The first she had ever seen apart from the childhood memory of a rabbit or two, certainly the first that she had seen for a long time.

Another day in the wood she saw a squirrel: lively, alert, agile beyond belief. She stopped and stared, watching the fascinating little creature in sheer delight until, less sure of itself than the fox, it caught sight of her and instantly sped up a tree and whisked round the bole into invisibility on the far side. So that Pentallan Great Wood became a place that she enjoyed, and although these days she came through it most mornings on her way to the Madeira-and-biscuit assignment with Charlie she never quite shook off the sense of mystery and even to some degree of awe that the silence of the place and the tall beech trees gave her.

At the Hall she didn't have to wonder whether she would

be welcome; it was becoming more and more obvious that Charlie was pleased to see her and that he looked forward eagerly to her now almost daily visit.

'In a way I miss Hooky Hefferman,' he said to her one morning, 'but I had to get rid of him, didn't I?'

'Of course you did.'

'I couldn't put up with the way he spoke to me, could I?'

'Of course you couldn't, Charlie.'

'And, anyway, I didn't need him anymore. He was quite useful at the very beginning when the press people were such a nuisance but, thank heavens, that's all died away now. I'm settled in now. I'm all right.'

'You're doing fine, Charlie.'

They were talking in the aviary at the end of the main drawing-room. Lately Dolly had taken an interest in the little birds and so Charlie's liking for them had revived and it had become normal, when Dolly called over to the Hall each morning, for them both to carry their glasses of Madeira to the aviary and watch the brightly coloured, noisy little creatures.

On these morning visits of Dolly Charlie's talk was nowadays almost invariably about the theatre. He had not yet been specifically asked for the twenty thousand pounds which he was 'going to be allowed to invest' in the new musical and the effect on him was remarkable. Dolly had a shrewd idea that the astute Jimmy Loader, much as he would have liked to have the money at once, was deliberately refraining from any suggestion of a hasty grab for fear of frightening his precious bird away. If this were so, Dolly had to acknowledge the effectiveness of the ploy. Every day Charlie's anxiety increased lest something had gone wrong and he wouldn't, after all, be given the chance of backing the show.

'Perhaps he will get the money from somewhere else.'

'He'll come to you for it, Charlie, don't worry.'

'It's not as though I'm really in the theatre world.'

'I keep telling you, Charlie, not to worry. Jimmy wants the money for the show and he'll come to you for it. All sorts of snags and delays happen in getting a show together, especially a musical. It will come out all right in the end.'

'Well, of course, I absolutely trust you, Dolly, you know that.'

'I wish you hadn't said that, Charlie,' the words slipped out before the woman could stop them and naturally enough they surprised their hearer.

'What on earth do you mean?' he asked.

She instantly regretted having said it and was sharper than she meant to be in her reply. 'Oh, nothing, nothing. You take everything so literally. You're too damn serious, Charlie boy.'

'Sorry. I always have been a bit on the solemn side. I'm afraid you must find me rather a bore.'

'I don't find you a bore at all, Charlie. Rather the contrary actually.'

Foolishly he returned to her original sentence. 'But about not saying I trusted – I don't understand that....'

This time she laughed at him. 'Forget it, Charlie. It was a nonsense. I was just thinking I have so often seen people trust others when they ought not to. That's all.'

'But this is different.'

She held out her glass and watched in silence whilst he refilled it with Madeira. 'Yes, maybe this is different,' she agreed at last.

It was not long before Charlie was asking her advice about matters concerning the Hall. 'Skipton says that all the kitchen quarters ought to be redecorated,' he told her one day. 'The butler's pantry and the passage leading to it and the kitchen itself and all the other bits and pieces. I'm sure he's right but would you have a look at it with me and say what you think I ought to do – paint or paper and what colours and so on?'

Intrigued by the request Dolly made a tour of the extensive territory lying on the other side of the green baize door. Skipton accompanied in wary attendance, and she was diplomatic enough to win him over by consulting his opinion and wishes at every turn. He treated her with punctilious politeness.

'Rather an old-fashioned set-up, I'm afraid, madam; but, then, I prefer it that way. Some of the modern stuff is all right. More convenient and so on. And some of it is a lot of nonsense in my opinion. Having a clutter-up of glass and chromium and fancy cupboards and such like doesn't necessarily mean you're going to run the house any better.'

'I'm sure you run this house very well indeed, Skipton.'

'Thank you, madam. Well, I do my best; I can say that. And I know how to do it; I can say that too. I'm a trained servant, madam, and I'm proud of it. Not the slapdash and skimping sort you get today.'

'Lord Pentallan is lucky to have you.'

'Since the very first day I came to his late Lordship I took a liking to this house, madam. To the Hall itself. I can't explain it exactly because, of course, it isn't what you would call a grand house. But there you are, I like it. I always wanted to see it look at its best. I'd like to see a proper establishment here, his Lordship married and so on, and entertaining people as we ought to.'

'Meanwhile we've got to get your kitchen quarters done up the way you want them.'

'I'm sure His Lordship will take any advice you give him about that, madam.'

Gradually Dolly slipped into the pleasant habit of staying on for lunch, which was always a welcome change from preparing a meal for herself. Sometimes this was impractical as Charlie would be going out; his uncle had been something of a recluse and it was only gradually that the new owner of the Hall was being caught up in the social round of the county. On one such morning Charlie urged her to stay on by herself and be looked after by Skipton. Dolly was tempted to accept the invitation, but without any clear reason in her head for doing so refused and walked back through the Great Wood and then down the Trackway to the cottage in Long Wood Lane.

When she went into her own kitchen the contrast between it and the comparatively vast arrangements up at the Hall amused her. Lunch would have to be a meagre meal and she had not bothered to go shopping for a day or two; but the excellent Mrs Penny had left everything faultlessly clean and tidy as usual, and Dolly began to examine what there was in the fridge and to decide what to get ready for herself. It looked as though it would have to be eggs and bacon, and afterwards she would go into Farnbridge to get something for the evening. She was in the act of putting the bacon under the grill when the front-door bell rang. For a second she lifted her head in surprise. Then she smiled slowly. Somehow she felt convinced that it was Charlie; his luncheon engagement must have fallen through and he had hurried back to carry her off to the Hall and the ministrations of Skipton. Dolly made a quick survey of her limited resources and was reassured. The eggs and bacon would be enough for two and (thank heaven!) there was a piece of really good Cheddar.

'I won't go up to the Hall,' she thought. 'I'll ask him to stay and we'll have lunch here.'

The bell rang again and she moved out of the kitchen and went to answer it. The man standing there said, 'How do you do, sister? I'm your brother Bertram just flown straight in by Jumbo Jet from Montreal.'

Dolly's reactions at so unexpectedly seeing Bunny on the doorstep of Gorse Cottage were extraordinarily mixed. Her first, instantaneous feeling was that she didn't want him there; more and more she was conscious of the need to be alone and to have time to think things out. Bunny belonged to the old life and his sudden appearance in these her new surroundings made her realise with startling abruptness how much she had been beginning to slough that old life off.

Yet the old life still had to be reckoned with; life caught up with you. Even if you wanted to, it wasn't all that easy to cut adrift from old habits and connections; Bunny was there and he had to be coped with. Her first response was a defensive one.

'You never telephoned and said you were coming.'

'You didn't either. Remember?' He smiled as he said it, but it wasn't altogether a friendly smile.

'So this is Gorse Cottage,' he continued, and without being invited he pushed his way past her into the tiny hall and so through into the living-room. Dolly followed him and said, 'I told you I would let you know when it was time to come down here.'

'Ah, but you haven't let me know, have you? The last time I rang it wasn't convenient to speak to me. You had somebody with you.'

'Charlie. Lord Pentallan.'

'Good. I hope you were working on him. Anyway, I thought I would come down and have a look for myself. I've been putting up the money, don't forget.'

'I'm not likely to the way you go on about it.'

He took a long look round the chintzy room and gave his verdict.

'Well, I suppose this is O.K., if you like this sort of thing.'

'I do like it. I wouldn't mind owning this cottage, I can tell you.'

'What size place is it? What have you got here?'

'There's this room and the kitchen beyond; then upstairs two bedrooms, a bathroom and a loo. There's nobody in the bedrooms, by the way. I haven't got a red-headed man in there putting his trousers on in a hurry.'

'O.K. O.K. Forget it, will you?' he flushed angrily. 'Just like a bloody woman to go on and on about a thing. You ought to have your precious Charlie up there in the bedroom. That would make some sense. Where is his Lordship by the way? Not going to have lunch with you? You haven't had lunch, have you?'

'I was just getting it when you rang the bell. Getting it for myself.'

'Count me in. Get it for the two of us.'

Dolly went back to the kitchen and got out two more rashers of bacon and two more eggs; in the living-room Bernard

Daley foraged round, discovered her small supply of drinks and helped himself.

Dolly knew her man pretty well and she realised that he was in one of his less tractable moods. He wouldn't have come down, she reasoned, unless he had a plan ready to be disclosed and discussed, and indeed his initial sentence when she had opened the door to him showed that he had such a plan; but in his contrary mood he was going to take his time about revealing it. She had noticed the same trait in him before: the better pleased he was with some plan that he had thought up the more circuitous was his approach in talking about it.

The meal, when it was served, didn't arouse any enthusiasm.

'Eggs and bacon? Not exactly the fat of the land, is it?'

Nevertheless, the eggs and bacon were eaten up with relish, and over the cup of coffee that followed the man seemed rather more relaxed.

Dolly watched him warily.

'Well, you're in the wilds here right enough,' he said. 'What do you do with yourself all day?'

'There always seems to be plenty to do.'

'Such as?'

'There's the garden for one thing.'

The man laughed incredulously. 'Don't tell me you've turned gardener,' he said.

'I'm beginning to take an interest in it. People change, you know, Bunny.'

He took a quick look at her and asked, 'Have you changed?'

'More coffee? Everyone changes.'

'And what about that boy friend of yours up at – what is it? – Pentallan Hall?'

'We've been seeing a lot of each other.'

'I should damn well hope so. That's what you're here for. That's what I've been dishing out the money for.'

'You're always on about the money.'

'Damn it, Dolly, it was you always on at me about not getting enough.'

'Those piddling bets of yours! I suppose you still go on with those every day.'

This angered him, and he answered sharply, 'That's like you. That's like a woman to keep picking on something that doesn't matter. Having something on every day is simply a game with me; it's my bit of fun. It doesn't matter whether I win or lose. It's just for the sport of it. You can't see that, of course, being a woman. When I'm in earnest, when a thing matters to me, I do it properly. I'm an artist. I want to turn in a good performance. As an actress you ought to appreciate that; well, when I say actress – *ex*-actress really. You aren't likely to be doing anything more in that line now, are you?'

'Why shouldn't I?'

'Come off it, Dolly. You've been out of it for – what is it? – six or seven years now. How do you imagine you could get back even if you wanted to? This is your game now; with me. You can do your bit of acting down here and give me the lead-in I want. You've been doing your homework, have you? You've got on all right with Pentallan?'

'We've become friendly. Yes.'

'Good for you. I knew you would work this end of it all right. He trusts you, does he?'

'He's a trusting sort of person.'

Bunny laughed. 'It's nice of Providence to make 'em that way,' he said. 'God supplies the pigeons and we pluck 'em. What could be fairer than that?'

Dolly poured out a second cup of coffee for herself, tasted it and then rejected it as being too cold. All this in silence. Finally she said, 'I take it you've thought up a scheme of some sort, then?'

Bunny leant back in his chair, gazed up at the ceiling and with evident self-satisfaction expounded his plan.

'If you go down to have a look in the list of registered companies you'll find the Montreal Mutual Investment and Property Development Holdings Limited among them. It's there for anyone to see. It exists. I registered it myself, and the fact that nobody else in the world knows anything about it, or is ever likely to, is neither here nor there. We keep that to ourselves. The *spiel* is this: I'm ex-Group Captain Bertram Leslie Dangerfield—'

'You've always been in the Army before.'

'This time I fancied the Air Force. Canadian Air Force. Virtually impossible for anyone here to check. I'm your brother. You haven't seen me since I emigrated to Canada years ago. In the meantime, what with one thing and another, we pretty well lost touch with one another. A letter once a year to let you know how I was doing was about the limit of it. And I've been doing very well. All the time you've been stuck here in England watching prices go up and opportunities go down I've been over in Canada where it's bigger and better and I've made good there. I've been made the General Manager of this huge company, the Montreal Mutual Investment and Property Development Holdings Limited; and we've made so much money that we are looking for somewhere else to expand. We are coming back to the Old Country to set up an English branch of the company here. We are quite certain that we can get all the money we want so we are not after anybody's cash—'

Dolly was forced to laugh. 'What will you tell him you are after, then?' she enquired.

'*I* shan't tell him anything. Not to start with. I don't know he exists. I'm straight from Montreal, Canada. *You'll* do the telling, Dolly. The way we are going to work the game is this: having come back to England after being away for years I naturally look up my sister – that's you. We were always fond of one another and you are delighted to see me and to hear all my news. Of course, I tell you all about how I have got on in Canada and the marvellous success of Mutual Investment and Property Development Holdings Limited and I also tell you why I am here. It's not cash we are looking for to get the company floated in England; it's a name for the board. We want a title. We shall have a strong board of directors, businessmen who know what it's all about; but we want a couple of names to attract the public and to assure everybody that it's all O.K. Window-dressing? Right, so it is; but window-dressing is a vital part of shopkeeping.

'Now, sister, I say to you, I've been out of England for years, away from all this business of titles and Lords. Where do you advise me to start looking for the sort of person we want?

'*That's* the story you take to your Charlie Pentallan. "Charlie," you tell him, "I haven't said a word about you to my brother yet, but as he was talking of course I was thinking of you all the time, so would you like me to mention your name?" Don't you think he'll fall for that?'

'Very likely he would. Charlie isn't what you would call a worldly-wise sort of person.'

'There's one born every minute and thank God for it.'

'It doesn't always work though, does it? It didn't work at Dalesford.'

'That's typical of you to remind me of that. But still you are quite right; something did go wrong at Dalesford. I've often thought about it and I'm damned if I can figure out what it was. I *know* when I've sold an idea to a sucker, when they've taken the bait; and that old lady pruning away at her roses fell for the yarn I spun her entirely. I'm sure she did. So what happened between my leaving her house and arriving at the bank?'

'Something might go wrong here.'

'Something can always go wrong. But that's no reason for not trying. And down here with the work you've already done and the *spiel* I've thought up and your putting it across we are on a good wicket. I'm sure of it.'

'You haven't said yet about getting anything out of it.'

'The first thing is for you to explain to your Lord Pentallan what *he* is going to get out of it. Always think of the customer first. You gather from me (you tell him) that people in the City are tumbling over themselves to get on the board of this Canadian company that's going to start up over here. Canada is the place; that's where the expansion is and where it's going to be for the next fifty years. Things are going to grow there, not contract like they are doing here. A seat on the board of the Mutual Investment and Property Development Holdings Limited is really something; it carries with it the automatic allotment of five thousand shares in the company: they are worth a lot now; in five years' time there's no telling what price they'll be quoted at – something fabulous. "So the Company gets your name and title, Charlie," you tell him, "and you very cleverly get yourself on to a red-hot good thing; naturally you can't expect a once-in-a-lifetime chance like that for nothing; the place on the board and the shares that go with it will cost you twenty thousand pounds cash and cheap at the price."'

'Twenty thousand!'

'Why not? You've always told me in the past that I haven't been ambitious enough. That was one of the things you said at Dalesford. I don't think you were right there. The set-up was entirely different. To talk about thousands to that old lady down there would have scared the life out of her: she would never have fallen for it. But here it's different. Here I reckon we can make a real killing. This is just about the ideal set-up: you've got the sucker lined up; he's got the money, plenty of it according to all accounts; and I've got the story. Of course, you'll have to wrap it up a good deal; lay it on thick about the need for speed and absolute secrecy; it's absolutely vital that no word of getting the board together for this new company should leak out into the City, and so on. And other men with titles are being considered so if Charlie doesn't want to be left out in the cold— You know the sort of thing.'

'I ought to. I've heard you putting it across often enough.'

'When are you next going to see this Charlie of yours – tomorrow?'

Dolly picked up a box of matches and lit a cigarette before answering, 'No, not tomorrow. He's away for a day or two.'

'Well, as soon as he's back, you get on with it and let me know on the blower how it's going. I can come down any time, of course. What about that chap Pentallan had to deal with the Press?'

'He's gone. He spoke out of turn and Charlie sent him packing.'

'That leaves a nice clear field for you, then, doesn't it? Just as soon as His Lordship gets back. Like I said, get cracking and let me know how he's taking it. What about the trains back to London from this part of the world and a taxi to the station. Can you lay that on?'

'You're not staying the night, then?'

'No. I want to be back at the flat.'

'Are you entertaining that cheap little redhead again?'

Daley flushed with anger, and for a moment Dolly thought he was going to hit her. She had hardly ever been scared of him before but now, for the instant, she was; for the instant he looked a meanly vicious little man.

But he swallowed his temper.

'You and I are working partners in this,' he said, 'and we are on to a good thing. If we work it right we are on to a very good thing indeed. Don't let's spoil it by falling out with one another, so just leave other things alone, will you?'

CHAPTER THIRTEEN

It was an immense relief when the taxi called to take Daley to Farnbridge Station and Dolly had the cottage to herself again. She went into the kitchen and set about washing-up the things used at luncheon, ruminating as she did so. Washing-up in the London flat had always been a tedious necessity, to be put off for as long as possible and got through with the minimum of effort. Here, in Gorse Cottage, it never seemed anything like as bad; she had come to terms with it, as she had learnt to come to terms with other things – the open fire and the garden – as part of the living-pattern of the cottage.

There was not a lot to do – four plates, some cutlery and a couple of glasses – and very soon everything was washed and dried and put away in its place, and the kitchen was in the spick and span state in which Mrs Penny always left it and in which Dolly had learnt to keep it.

Dolly did the work slowly for she found that she had a lot to think about. Bunny's plan was a good one; no doubt about that. Whatever happened in the future, she would always be prepared to admit that he was a first-rate con man. To be a good con man you had to be a good psychologist; you had to be able to size people up and to realise what made them tick and where their weak spots were.

It was clear that, even without having met Charlie, Bunny had made a pretty shrewd assessment of the position. Dolly felt unhappily sure that if she put the scheme up to Charlie in the way she had been told it would succeed. She could make Charlie fall for it; and in a few weeks' time she and

Bunny would be twenty thousand pounds better off.

What had made Bunny fix on that particular sum, she wondered, uncharacteristically ambitious for him? She supposed that, ironically enough, she herself was responsible; that her taunts on previous occasions about the smallness of the targets he set himself had decided him to go for something big this time. It was impossible not to be struck by the oddness of the coincidence between the two amounts – the twenty-thousand-pound swindle thought up by Bunny and the twenty-thousand-pound backing asked for by Jimmy Loader. She tried to argue with herself that a man who had inherited the sort of money Charlie Pentallan had come into wouldn't really mind whether he got rid of twenty or forty thousand of it.

Thus she argued; but she didn't convince herself. She remembered that Charlie had surprised her on one occasion by talking about trusts and settlements and entails, matters which she only vaguely understood, and by hinting that when it came to ready cash there wasn't all that much available. And there was something more.... The work in the kitchen was finished and she was now standing in front of the open fire in the living-room, the room in which recently Bernard Daley had been sitting telling her what his plan was and what her part in it was to be; now she was alone and the room was hers again. She lit a cigarette and flicked the match into the fire. There was something more. It had been forming at the back of her mind for some time and now it refused to be unacknowledged any longer – the something was the simple fact she didn't want to swindle Charlie Pentallan. Whether he could afford to lose the money or not she found that she didn't want to have a hand in taking it off him. It was a relief to realise the thought and to get it crystallised and formulated at last. But if it was a relief it was also something of a bewilderment. Six years ago it had seemed smart to team up with a clever con man and it had actually been fun to use her dramatic talents – which the theatre didn't seem to want – in helping him with his *coups*; now— What the hell has happened to me? she said, half to herself, half aloud, as she moved slowly across the room and looked out on to the garden and the trees beyond.

Her statement to Bunny about Charlie being away for some days was not true, of course; it had been a delaying tactic, instinctively adopted as a defence against something which, as she was now prepared to acknowledge to herself, she didn't want to do.

She was, in fact, due to go to the Hall on the following day as she explained next morning to Mrs Penny.

'And do you want me to get something ready for your lunch?' Mrs Penny enquired. 'Some potatoes or something?'

'No. I don't think so, Mrs Penny. I shan't be in for lunch.'

'You'll be going up to the Hall likely?'

'Yes, Lord Pentallan has asked me to go up there and have lunch with him; and I must say it's rather better fun than eating alone here.'

' 'Course it is. My goodness, if I had to sit down day after day and eat all by myself I don't know how I should stand it. Penny isn't in midday, of course; I put up some sandwiches for him to take to the job and he comes home for his dinner five o'clock and, my word, he wants it. But I've the three little ones; well, I say little, but they aren't all that little now, they're all growing up; they come home from school for their midday meal and aren't they just hungry. Of course, with three of them to feed and get ready for, there's plenty to do, but who minds that, not really minds. I'd sooner have six of them than sit down solemn by myself.'

Dolly laughed and said, 'With a husband and three children you must have your hands pretty full.'

'Yes, I do,' Mrs Penny agreed, 'and, do you know, Mrs Acton, I reckon that's what a woman's hands are for. There's a piece in the Bible about the everlasting arms. Whenever I hear that read out I think it means a woman's arms. Holding everything up, her man and her children; doing things for them. Yes, I reckon empty hands mean an empty heart. And that's no good to anybody, is it?'

'Not much,' Dolly admitted dryly.

'And how does His Lordship feed you up at the Hall?'

'Oh, it varies, you know. Sometimes good, sometimes not so good.'

'I reckon what he wants is a woman's hand up there. A house needs a woman to do the managing of it.'

When Dolly arrived at the Hall Charlie was sitting at his desk dealing with correspondence. He welcomed Dolly's entrance into the room by holding a letter aloft and waving excitedly.

'I've heard from your friend Jimmy Loader at last. He says it's all right for me to put the money in now, so I'm just about to write the cheque.'

'You're sure you want to do it, Charlie?'

'Of course I want to do it; it's an absolutely marvellous chance.'

'As long as you realise that there's no such thing as a theatrical certainty; there's always a certain amount of risk.'

'There's a risk about everything; but look at *Purple Evening*. Isn't that doing well?'

'Fabulously, from all accounts.'

'Anyone lucky enough to have put money in that will make a fortune surely?'

Dolly nodded and was forced to smile at his enthusiasm.

'Yes, they very likely will,' she agreed.

'There you are, then; the more I can get back for my twenty thousand the better pleased I shall be, obviously; but it isn't only that; it isn't only the money; it's the fun of being caught up in a world I never dreamed I would have anything to do with. Of course, I'm telling Loader in my letter that part of the bargain is that he does what he said he would – gives you a part in the show.'

'Well, you know how I feel about that, Charlie.'

'I don't know that I do. I often wonder what your feelings are about a number of things, Dolly. Tell me how you feel about having a part in the new musical.'

'Tremendously excited and frightfully scared. But the

excitement beats the scare – just. It's difficult to explain – I expect it's difficult for outsiders to understand – but once you've been part of the theatre, once you've been in a show, you never really get it out of your blood. It's a world on its own, Charlie—'

'I realise that. I know it is and I'm going to belong to it in a way.'

'Of course you are, of course you are.'

'Once you get started again, Dolly, I'm sure you won't be scared. I can't imagine you being scared of anything. How long is it since you were in a play?'

Dolly thought for a moment and then said, 'It's almost exactly seven years since I had a part in a play, a revival of Priestley's *The Linden Tree.*'

'And you haven't done any acting at all in the meantime?'

Dolly took even longer about answering that question. At length she laughed and made an odd little gesture with her hands. The man listening to her understood neither the quality of the laugh nor the significance of the gesture.

'No. No acting. Not what anyone in their senses would call acting. And that doesn't mean anything either, Charlie. Forget it. I've done nothing. I've just been a fool. Send your cheque off to Jimmy Loader and we will all go on our knees and pray like mad that Sherlock Holmes is a success, a smash hit. It could be; I really believe that.'

'What was your stage name, Dolly?'

'Bennett. Dolly Bennett.'

'And how long ago is it since Ben walked out on you?'

Dolly's thoughts were running strongly on matters of the theatre and for a moment she was at a loss.

'Ben?'

'The man you married.'

'Oh, *Ben*—'

'You told me he deserted you, just walked off—'

'So I did. I'd forgotten; I mean I wasn't thinking for the moment.'

She crossed the room to the table by the window and said,

'Can I pour myself out a drink?'

Slightly surprised, he told her yes, of course, anything she wanted.

She poured whisky into a tumbler and added a splash of soda. The ploy was made in order to give herself time to think more than for any other reason. Eventually she turned and faced him and said, 'Charlie, forget about Ben.'

'Forget about him?'

She took a gulp of her drink, having realised suddenly that even now she was only going to tell half the truth. Was half going to be better or worse than nothing? She didn't know.

'We weren't married....'

He was watching her curiously, waiting for her to go on. Now she wished she had never started any sort of explanation – better to leave the lie as it was – but she *had* started so she had better go on, making up as she went along; she just wished to God Charlie wouldn't look at her in that innocent, trusting way. She realised that having said so much she would have to round things off. She hustled her words out. 'There's no story really. Nothing to it. We lived together and then off he went. We weren't married, but people had got in the way of calling me Mrs Acton and when I came down here to see about taking the cottage I thought a married woman would stand more chance of getting it than somebody single. People might have thought I had designs on you, Charlie. So that's all there is to it. I'm not married and never have been. If you like, you can say I'm playing a part and Mrs Acton is the name of the part.'

The man listening didn't quite know what to make of all this; he didn't get the drift of it; but at least it produced one simple and uncomplicated reaction from him.

'I'm glad you're not married, Dolly,' he said.

They had lunch together and Dolly thought with some amusement that she must remember to report to Mrs Penny that Mrs Skipton had excelled herself – cold roast beef, incredibly tender, and an apple pie baked by a master hand.

After lunch Charlie announced that he had to walk over to one of the two Pentallan farms and in his hesitant, almost apologetic way suggested that she might like to go with him.

'Of course I should like to go.'

'It won't bore you?'

'Not in the slightest.'

'I always think of you as a smart town-person somehow.'

Dolly laughed and made a gesture almost it might seem of surrender.

'That's how I used to think of myself, Charlie. I used to think London was the only place; everything beyond Shepherd's Bush was the Wild West and north of Islington was the Arctic wasteland. I expect I shall think like that again when I go back there to live; but for the present I'm enjoying being in the country.'

'You'll have to try to buy Gorse Cottage from Major Fellows when he comes back. Wasn't it an extraordinary thing that he should have been an old friend of yours and own a cottage almost next door to Pentallan Hall?'

'Coincidences happen all the time.'

'Where did you and he first get to know one another?'

'Oh, I've no idea. I forget. I don't write everything down in a diary. Anyway, that's over; that all belongs to the past. Now I'm living in the present. Here. Gorse Cottage and Pentallan Great Wood and going to walk with you to whereever it is you are taking me. Let's forget about the past, for God's sake.'

The irritation in her voice took him by surprise and he looked crestfallen. Seeing this Dolly felt assailed by annoyance, amusement and compassion in about equal proportions.

'Now, stop worrying, Charlie,' she said, 'and tell me what it is you are taking me to see.'

In its hey-day the Pentallan estate had consisted of some eight thousand acres, a good deal of it enclosed within the 'ring fence' so highly prized by our property-conscious forebears. Through three successive generations the family had moved out of land and into the City, in which process they acquired a lot of money and got rid of the greater part of their property. Nowadays only just over fifteen hundred acres was left – 'And that's quite enough to have to worry about with taxation and everything the way it is,' Charlie complained as they were on their way; but he said it happily, with all the enthusiasm of a child for a new toy in his voice.

Dolly said that fifteen hundred acres sounded a lot to her.

'Not that much, really. There are two farms – Pentallan Home Farm which is something over four hundred acres; Mockbeggar Farm which is twice as big and then there are four cottages and the Pentallan Arms and the Hall itself, of course.'

'Do you own the Pentallan Arms, Charlie?'

'It's part of the estate.'

'So every time I have a drink there I'm doing you a good turn?'

'Not really. The estate doesn't get the profits from it. Just the rent. It's let to the brewery.'

By now they had emerged on the far side of the Great Wood and were following the headland which skirted a large ploughed field.

'This is one of the Mockbeggar Farm fields,' Charlie said. 'I'm getting to know all the property gradually.'

'Mockbeggar Farm – what a marvellous name.'

'I suppose it looks rather grand and in the days when there were lots of beggars about anyone seeing it across the fields – there it is now, look – might have thought it was the big house of the district and gone trudging all the way up the cart-road to it hoping for a hand-out only to find when he got up there a busy farmer's wife who didn't mind saying in round terms that she had no use for layabouts.'

At Mockbeggar Farm the matter that had to be considered was the necessity of repairs to one of the great barn doors which had been damaged in a gale some months before. They were shown the problem and then escorted round the farm buildings generally by an elderly, gravely courteous man who was intrigued to know what Dolly's standing might be but much too polite to let his curiosity be seen.

As they came away Charlie said, 'Well, there you are. It will cost all of fifty pounds to get that barn door repaired properly. But one has to do it, of course. And I must say it's better fun having a whole, complete little world of one's own to care about and look after.'

During the days that followed Dolly was worried by a fear which common sense told her was irrational but which nevertheless she still allowed to bother her – the fear that Bernard Daley would appear again at Gorse Cottage. Unannounced, of course, as he had come the first time; and, as far as she was concerned, unwanted. She found it difficult to explain, even to herself, why; or to pinpoint the exact moment when her mind had shifted in the matter; but the fact was that now she wanted to be finished with Bernard Daley. Looking back over their partnership she could see that as far as she was concerned disenchantment had begun some time ago, even before the unsuccessful affair at Dalesford; now she was asking herself in dismay and bewilderment how in God's name she had ever become mixed up with him at all. She still considered Daley to be in many ways a weak character; but weak characters, she was beginning to learn, could turn vicious, and she was not at all happy about what might happen when she announced that the working partnership was finished and the Pentallan *coup* wasn't going to take place. Like most people faced with the probability of unpleasant possibilities sometime in the future she continued not to think about it too much and to concentrate on the present.

More than ever Gorse Cottage, with friendly Pentallan Hall hard by, took on the aspect of home for her, a retreat where she hoped that the things she wanted to be finished with wouldn't catch up with her.

She told Mrs Penny about the visit to Mockbeggar Farm and they laughed together over the oddity of the name. Mrs Penny knew all about the Pentallan estate and still retained a lot of interest in it because her father as a young man had been estate carpenter.

'What happened to him?' Dolly enquired.

'Well, the money wasn't much in those days and the family began to sell off the land, and Dad thought that presently there wouldn't be any work for him and he might get sold off as well, so he set up in Farnbridge in a carrier and odd-jobs business. It was up and down, some years better than others, but we managed; and I will say this, nobody had a kinder, happier home than I did. Right up till the day he died Dad always took an interest in the estate; in a way I think he was always a bit sorry he left. Of course, it's nothing like the size it used to be. There are only the two farms now; but it would be nice to see everything as it should be up at the Hall again.

'Come to that, village life has changed, too, since I was a girl; oh, my word, changed out of all recognition. Everybody used to know everybody, and everybody else's business, too, I can tell you! You walk up the village street today you hardly know a soul. We're all a lot of strangers. Mind you, it's better in some ways; people are more independent and there's more money about, but still – oh, well, no use looking back on the past all the time, is it?'

'Not the slightest,' Dolly agreed.

'Of course, some things go on the same. We've still got the Fête. Will you be here for that, Mrs Acton? June the first and second?'

'Yes, I expect I shall still be here then. Tell me about the Fête.'

'It used to be bigger; there was more to it, like; but everybody still looks forward to it. It's always two days, Saturday and Sunday. On Saturday the Hall gardens are open and people walk round and have a look at everything; of course, it's no good pretending they are what they used to be when there were six gardeners kept, but still there's always something to look at, and the Pentallan maze is quite famous. The maze and the rhododendrons are the things; people come from miles to see them.

'Then on Sunday it's the cricket match. That's been going on for I don't know how long. The village against a visiting team. For the past few years Tom Pacey of the Arms has been in charge of that. My word, he's just about cricketing mad is Tom Pacey. When there's one of these Test matches on in Australia they say Tom never gets a wink of sleep all night trying to listen in to it on the radio. I can't see any sense in it myself, but that's how men go on. Childish in lots of ways, aren't they, Mrs Acton? What I like best at the Fête is the fortune teller.'

Dolly pricked up her ears when a fortune teller was mentioned; she thought of Madame Vana.

'I always go to her,' Mrs Penny was continuing. 'I know it's silly, but there you are. Men are silly about their games and I'm silly about having my fortune told. You tell her what sign you are, you know, according to your birthday and she tells you your character and what's likely to happen to you. I'm Leo. Which sign are you, Mrs Acton?'

'My birthday's next week. May the twenty-first. That's Taurus, isn't it?'

'Yes, Taurus. Funny, I wouldn't have thought of you as Taurus. You can never tell with people, though, can you?'

Dolly was forced to laugh at that piece of homely wisdom; no, she agreed, you could never tell with people.

Four days after her talk with Mrs Penny about the forthcoming fête she was bidden to the Hall again, this time not for lunch but in the evening.

She didn't know whether other guests were going to be there or not and was undecided about what to wear – long dress as for something of an occasion, or short for easy-going informality? In the end she remembered the advice of the first producer she had ever worked with in her theatrical days – 'Always dress up, my dear, even if you are only going out to the post; it always pays a woman to look her best' – and she chose her full-length black with the flowing sleeves. All doubts as to whether she was right or not were dispelled the moment she was shown into the Pentallan drawing-room by Skipton and Charlie caught sight of her.

'What a marvellous dress,' he cried. 'You look absolutely super in it.'

Dolly laughed at his boyish enthusiasm but it was balm to her woman's ears.

'I haven't asked anybody else,' Charlie said, 'so it isn't really a party. Do you mind that?'

'I'm bitterly disappointed, Charlie' – but her eyes smiled at him. In the dining-room it looked as though the first course was already served. Covers were in position in the two laid places. Keeping the starter hot, Dolly assumed, until Skipton with the air of a willing conspirator whipped her cover away and she found herself looking at a small package and a large card.

'Happy Birthday,' it said.

She looked up and met Charlie's excited eyes.

'How on earth did you know?' she asked.

'Village grape-vine. Your Mrs Penny and my Mrs Skipton both belong to the Women's Institute. The W.I. had their usual meeting last Friday and Mrs Skipton happened to say that, talking about fortune tellers and so on, you had mentioned that your birthday was on May the twenty-first—'

'I had no idea that Mrs Penny would tell anybody; it was just in the way of conversation; we were talking about the signs of the Zodiac—'

'Taurus.'

'Yes, Taurus. Mrs Penny didn't seem to think it suited me.'

'See if that suits you.' Charlie indicated the small package lying on Dolly's plate. 'I went up to London this morning to get it.'

Dolly opened the small, oblong box and found herself looking at what was obviously an expensive brooch, an oval-shaped emerald set in tiny diamonds. She stared at it in inward dismay. Of its quality there could be no doubt, and many women would have thought it lovely. Dolly herself was prepared to agree that it was lovely, but it was also an emerald and it was green, and about emeralds and the colour green she was incurably superstitious. For a moment she didn't know what to say; finally she said what any woman would have done in the circumstances.

'Oh, Charlie, you shouldn't have—'

'Do you like it?'

'Of course I like it. It's marvellous.'

'I expect you've got plenty of jewellery already.'

'No, indeed I haven't.'

'Well, you're the sort of woman who ought to have. A beautiful woman ought to have beautiful things.'

The May evening was so warm that after dinner they moved out on to the terrace and Skipton brought them their coffee there. The gentle English twilight lay over the gardens; some distance off a tractor could just be heard working late in one of the Mockbeggar Farm hayfields; in the foreground the thick yew hedges of the maze were beginning to be indistinctly dark. It was a peaceful and secure-looking scene.

'Rather pleasant sitting here, looking out over it all, isn't it?' Lord Pentallan said.

'Very.'

'More coffee?'

'No, no more, thank you.'

The man poured out a second cup of coffee for himself and then gave an unexpected twist to the conversation.

'Do you believe in fate, Dolly?' he asked.

'In fate?' The question surprised and even startled her a little. 'Yes, I do. Very much so, in fact. What makes you ask that?'

'Well, I've been thinking a good deal about it lately, and it does really seem rather extraordinary that we should have met that time at Maidenhead and then, years later, you should happen to be a friend of Colonel Fellows and rent Gorse Cottage from him without the ghost of a notion that you were going to find yourself next door to me. Don't you agree that that's really a bit remarkable? I believe there's a pattern in the way things work out, don't you?'

She was immensely relieved to be asked a question she could answer openly and sincerely.

'Yes, I believe that, Charlie, I do believe that.'

'I hope the pattern is going to work out all right for Sherlock Holmes!'

Dolly laughed. 'Yes, indeed. Oh, Charlie, isn't it exciting, having that to look forward to?'

'It's the second most exciting thing that's happened to me in my life.'

'The second? What's the first?' For once her thoughts were slower than his and she asked the question in all innocence.

'Meeting you, Dolly.'

Charlie paused for a moment before going on, then he gave a little laugh and said, 'I've often thought back to that evening at Maidenhead and wondered what sort of impression you got of me. I'm afraid you must have thought me pretty naïve – a bit of a young ass, I suppose. Which I dare say I was in some ways; we don't all grow up at the same rate, do we? But even then I knew what I thought about you, Dolly; and now that we are – what is it? – twelve years older, and this extraordinary chance has happened that we have met again I still think it. Only more so. I think that you are the most wonderful person in the world. Twelve years ago I was still at Oxford; I hadn't got anything. Now I've got a home and some sort of position. There's only one person I want to share them with, Dolly, and that's you.'

There was quite a long silence whilst the woman looked out over the peaceful English garden, her thoughts a tumult within her.

'So now you know,' Charlie went on, 'why I was so glad when you told me that you weren't really married at all.'

When she answered Dolly spoke slowly and with uncharacteristic hesitation in her voice.

'But first of all, Charlie, I told you that I was married. I came here as Mrs Acton. I lied to you.'

'I suppose no one tells the strict truth all the time. The point is that you are *not* married and I'm now asking you to be. And don't be afraid that it will interfere with your theatre work because it needn't. I won't let it. In fact, by being ready to back shows from time to time I could probably be a help to you.'

'Charlie, I'm older than you are, you know—'

The man laughed happily. 'Oh, Dolly, darling,' he exclaimed, 'don't think up silly reasons why *not*, just say you *will*. Of course, I quite see that you may not want to say it straight away, this minute. You will want to think things over. And we are not living a hundred miles away from one another, are we?'

Dolly clutched at the straw. 'Yes, I'd like to think things over a bit, Charlie,' she said.

Because of being in her long, black evening dress she had hired the village taxi to bring her from Gorse Cottage and it had appeared faithfully on time to take her back again. She paid it off at the gate, and Gloriana emerged from the darkness of the tiny front garden to greet her. When she went in, the now familiar cottage felt friendly and welcoming; she went straight up to her bedroom and, having laid the green emerald brooch carefully on the dressing-table, began the ritual of getting ready for bed.

She was sitting in front of the mirror brushing her hair when the telephone rang. Charlie to say 'good-night'? she wondered as she went to the instrument.

It wasn't Charlie wishing to say 'good-night'; it was Bernard Daley angry and, she guessed, in liquor.

'About time,' he started as soon as he heard her answering 'Hallo'. 'Where the hell have you been? This is the fourth time I've tried to get you this evening.'

Bunny drunk was invariably objectionable as the woman well knew from experience; in any case, at that particular moment she had no desire to talk to him drunk or sober.

'There's a place called Pentallan Hall,' she answered with heavy sarcasm. 'You may have heard of it. I've been dining there.'

'A good job, too. You ought to have that young fool up

there properly on the hook by now. Why the hell haven't you rung me?'

'You always say not to spoil things by hurrying, Bunny.'

'I suppose you are having a damned good time in that cottage of yours. That's the truth of it, isn't it?'

'What do you expect me to do? Go about in sackcloth and ashes?'

'I expect you to get on with things and to let me know what's happening.'

'Have you been drinking, Bunny?'

'Mind your own god-damned business.'

'I only hope you're not too pissed to use a bit of common sense.'

'What do you mean? Have you put the *spiel* I told you about up to Pentallan or not?'

'Of course I've put it up to him and he has fallen for it completely. I've got him thinking Canada is the only place worth investing in.'

'If all that's true, what's the hold-up? I can come down straight away.'

'If you do you'll spoil everything.'

'Why, what's the snag?'

'Twenty thousand pounds is a lot of money.'

'It isn't all that much to somebody who has come into a million plus.'

'He has come into the title and the estate, yes; but surely you aren't too tight to realise that with a will of that amount there are a hell of a lot of legal formalities and complications. I don't pretend to understand it all – trusts and settlements and things like that; the point is that you want cash, and at the moment the actual cash isn't there. Of course, it *will* be there, but at the moment it isn't – or is that too complicated for you to understand at this time of night?'

'As long as it's there in the end—'

'Of course it will be there in the end; didn't you see in the papers how much he came in for?'

'Well, don't let it be too long before I hear something from you.'

'As soon as ever the time's right I'll let you know.'

'You mind you do.'

The woman put the receiver back on the bedside instrument and sat for several minutes in thought; then she crossed to the dressing-table and picked up the birthday present Lord Pentallan had given her; she turned it this way and that, studying it, fascinated by the way the light flashed back from the brilliance of its setting; she wished it had not been an emerald, she wished that it wasn't green; finally she smiled slightly. 'I think that you are the most wonderful person in the world.' Charlie's words came back to her; she put the brooch down carefully. After all, when I am Lady Pentallan, she thought, there will be other jewellery to wear.

CHAPTER FOURTEEN

It was perfectly true that Bernard Daley was not sober when he made the late-night telephone-call to Gorse Cottage, but drunk or sober he was a professional; in the past he himself had often counselled his partners (Dolly among them) against being in too much of a hurry. 'Softlee softlee catchee monkey,' he was wont to say. 'No sense in jumping at things; you'll only frighten the bird away.' So now he felt obliged to agree that there was sense in what Dolly had told him; and provided that she was still consolidating the necessary groundwork he was prepared to bide his time.

He was prepared to bide his time – for a time. In spite of Dolly's assurances and his own realisation that being in too much of a hurry might easily be counter-productive there was a small, nagging doubt at the back of his mind which refused to disappear; he didn't see just how or why things shouldn't work out right but he couldn't altogether get rid of the feeling that there might be something wrong somewhere.

'I'll give it another week or two,' Daley told himself, 'and then, by God, I'll want to hear that things are moving a bit.'

Giving it another week or two was an easy decision to make because the bedroom in the Marble Arch flat which Dolly had liked to consider her own was now permanently occupied by someone else. The cheap little redhead who had been a casual pick-up, and, as it turned out, an unsatisfactory one, had gone; and her place taken by someone who was proving much more to Daley's liking. In almost every way she was the direct antithesis of Dolly Bennett, and in a rare moment of self-analysis Daley realised that this difference was the very reason why he found the newcomer so attractive.

She was submissive, where Dolly had always been high-handed and imperious; she was avid for sex, and Dolly had never shown much enthusiasm for it; she welcomed Daley's whims and fancies in bed, which Dolly had always contemptuously denied him. Dolly was necessary to the scheme in hand, but it suited Daley to have her out of the way for at least a little longer. What would happen when she eventually came back on the scene was anybody's guess, and for the moment he refused to worry about it overmuch. There would be one hell of a row, of course, trust the Duchess (his own derisive private nickname for Dolly) for that; but on the other hand there would be twenty thousand pounds to play with and, he assured himself with a vicious little chuckle, if Dolly didn't behave herself she would find that her share of the booty was a mighty small one.

Meanwhile he was enjoying himself; his new companion, who at first acquaintance had seemed so demure and self-effacing, turned out to be almost as demanding about being entertained as she was in bed. Every evening she wanted the noise and lights and company of a pub for an hour or two before going back with Daley to the flat. More than one barman, watching the quietly spoken, modestly behaved little figure, wondered where the hell she put all the gin and how she managed to carry it. As a result of his companion's drinking habits Daley himself was drinking a great deal more; by the sort of logic which men tend to employ in such cases he easily persuaded himself that it was Dolly who had inhibited his drinking in the past (whereas, in fact, she had been rather contemptuous of his frugality) and that this was one more instance of his freedom under the new dispensation.

They had a round of three or four pubs which they visited according to what mood they were in, but it was the Black Boy in Bartholomew Mews – quite close to the flat – which they tended to use most.

On the first Saturday after Daley's telephone call to Gorse Cottage he was in the Black Boy ordering the second round of drinks and looking forward to an agreeable hour or so before going back to the flat for an even more agreeable session in bed.

'A large gin and water,' he said, 'and a Scotch and soda.' His companion never drank anything but gin and water, didn't seem to have heard of anything smaller than a double.

The Boy was pleasantly full. It was a pub which didn't have, as many pubs do, a hard core of faithful regulars; it seemed rather to attract people from a wide area and to thrive on a shifting population. On this particular Saturday night a group of four men came into the bar just as Daley was settling down in his seat with the drinks. His companion caught sight of them and was immediately interested.

'Why, there's Jimmy Loader!' she cried.

'And who's Jimmy Loader?'

'The theatrical man. Everybody knows Jimmy. I did a bit of modelling through him once, only I didn't really have the right measurements. Jimmy!'

Jimmy Loader, relaxed for once and in a cheerful mood, heard his name called and looked across the room. He half-recognised the face, but couldn't quite put a name to it; some bit-part actress, or more likely would-be actress, he supposed; still you never knew, always useful to keep in with people; and, after all, it was Saturday night, no harm in saying hallo.

He came across. 'Hallo there,' he said amiably. (Eve? Evelyn? Eva? He couldn't quite fix it.) 'How's tricks?'

'So so, Jimmy.'

'Working now?'

'Resting, Jimmy. Enjoying myself. Having a good time.' Her foot sought and pressed Daley's under the table.

'Sensible girl.'

'I hear you're busy, Jimmy.'

'Busy?' He made a semi-humorous gesture. 'They'll have me in my grave before they've finished with me.'

'A new musical, isn't it? Didn't I read about it in the *Stage*?'

'That's it. Sherlock Holmes. Ever heard of him?'

'Of course I have. I'm not sure exactly what he was, but everybody knows the name.'

Jimmy was delighted. 'There you are, then. Everybody will come to the show, won't they?'

'When do you open, Jimmy?'

'Don't worry; we'll open O.K. I'll tell everyone the date before long. And we've got everything fixed, cast, score, lyrics, the lot. And at last enough finance to get it going. There's a certain gentleman willing to give me the extra bit I wanted. Mind you, he's on to a good thing; and, in any case, he can afford it, he's just come into a little matter of a million and a quarter. His father or uncle or somebody fell down dead in one of the West End clubs a couple of months back, did you read about it?'

Eva shook her head.

'Lord Pentallan, do you mean?' Daley asked in a quiet voice.

'Pentallan. That's the chap. Pentallan Hall he lives in now. In the country somewhere. I've got a little friend of mine – well, actually, she's got a part in the show – who's got a cottage nearby; she has palled up with His Lordship and persuaded him to become a patron of the arts.' Jimmy laid a finger to one side of his nose and gave a knowing little laugh; he was in great good spirits. 'And that's the way the world goes, isn't it?' he said.

'Good luck to you, Jimmy,' Eva said. 'You always did know your way around.'

'You say this friend of yours has persuaded Lord Pentallan to put up the money for your musical?' Daley asked; he was now extremely sober.

'Well, twenty thousand quid of it, anyway.'

'Twenty thousand pounds?' Daley repeated the words wonderingly and stared at the speaker of them.

'And, believe me, he'll get it all back, with interest,' Jimmy declared. 'This one's going to be a smash hit.'

Shortly after nine next morning Eva was wakened from

drowsy half-sleep by the noises of Daley moving about in the bedroom. On any Sunday morning it would have been unusual for either of them to be stirring at that time, and after the sort of night they had had she was astonished to see him getting up so early.

'What time is it?' she asked sleepily.

'Just gone nine – five, ten past.'

'What's the hurry? What are you getting up for?'

'I'm going off for the day; into the country.'

She sat up, tousle-headed; protesting; half-feigning, half-meaning indignation.

'Aren't I coming with you?'

'Not this time.'

'You're going to leave me alone all day?'

'Don't worry. I'll be back. I've got a bit of business to get settled up; then I'll be back.'

On Saturday, 1 June, 'Fête Saturday' as it was generally called in the village, Tom Pacey and his wife were kept busy all day in the Pentallan Arms. The astonishing weather-luck which the Fête had enjoyed for years held yet again, and although there had been rain early on it troubled nobody. 'Rain before seven, fine before eleven,' the wiseacres assured one another, and so it turned out. By eleven o'clock white clouds were moving lazily across a blue sky and the sun was shining brilliantly.

By midday the first coachload of visitors had arrived, and before they went to look at the Hall, the gardens and the maze most of them called in at the Pentallan Arms. Tom Pacey thought the fête a first-rate idea; it was good for business. If people wanted to look at the gardens or spend money on the various sideshows and the fortune teller, let them. There was more money than sense about these days, the honest publican was convinced, and as long as they had some over to get rid of in the Arms he was content; but busy though Saturday made him, and beneficial to his till though it might be, the really important part of the week-end, as far as Tom was concerned, was the cricket match on Sunday.

All through Saturday morning, whenever he could snatch a moment away from a busy bar, he was contacting either by telephone or messenger various members of his team to make sure that they would be on duty at twelve the following day.

As usual his wife viewed it all with a mixture of scorn and amused impatience.

'This blessed old cricket of yours. Anyone would think it really mattered,' she cried.

'Matters? Well, of course it matters.'

'Children, that's what men are. They've no more sense than a lot of children.'

'Can't have,' Tom agreed, 'to put up with some of the wives we get.' He gave his wife a quick kiss to take any sting out of the remark and went on, 'All the local lads are O.K.; they'll turn up. The one I'm worried about is Mr Hefferman.'

'Why worry? Even if he doesn't come you can always get one extra out of the village, can't you? There's plenty want to play.'

'There isn't plenty been opening bats for the Free Foresters.'

'What's that? A sort of friendly society or something?'

Tom Pacey shook his head in despair. Women, he thought. You couldn't get on without 'em; of course not, no man could; salt of the earth in some ways; but, by God, there were some things they would never learn about!

'Still, I think he'll come,' the landlord went on. 'He told me he would and by my reckoning he's a sportsman and a gentleman. He's got a sense of what's right has Mr Hefferman.'

'He's also got a roving eye,' Tom's wife reminded him. 'If there's a pretty girl bobbed up on the scene in the meantime I don't suppose your opening bat and Free Forester business would stand much chance.'

Her husband affected not to have heard the treacherous words spoken so lightheartedly.

Shortly before one o'clock, when the Saturday-morning

trade was at its height, Hooky parked his beloved Jag in the forecourt of the Arms and, ducking his head to clear the low doorway, walked into the crowded bar.

'I suppose you were getting nervous I wasn't going to turn up?' he said to Tom Pacey.

'Never doubted it, sir; never doubted it for a minute. Never crossed my mind.'

'Don't believe a word he says,' Mrs Pacey put in. 'Tom's been as jumpy as a kitten all morning; he said he was afraid if you met a pretty girl you might go off with her instead of thinking about being an opening bat or whatever it is.'

'May God forgive her,' Tom said. 'Don't believe a word she's saying, Mr Hefferman. Don't believe a word of it.'

Hooky smiled amiably and answered, 'I thought the most attractive woman I was likely to see would be the one behind the bar at the Pentallan Arms just about to mix a Pimms No. 1 for me. How about it, Mrs Pacey?'

Mary Pacey dropped her eyes and coloured slightly. 'I'll mix one for you now,' she said.

One hour and a half and several Pimms later Hooky in bucolic mood set out to sample the delights of a rustic fête. The Hall gardens had been impressively tidied up and prepared for the occasion; the rock gardens, the lily pond and the one huge border were certainly all worth looking at, but the two things which interested people most were the maze, which was astonishing in its size and intricacy, and the great bank of summer flowering rhododendrons, a rarity in those parts and something which keen gardeners from far and wide were always eager to see.

In addition to this pleasant backcloth, largely provided by nature, there were the less aesthetically pleasing but, for Hooky at any rate, more interesting works of man – the various tents and sideshows which had been set up on the lower lawn and in the paddock beyond it. The traditional things without which no village fête would really be a fête were all there – the Roll-'em-in, the Coconut Shy, the Bowling for a Pig, the Shooting Gallery, the White Elephant Stall, the

Bottle Stall, the Fortune Teller's Tent, the Tea Tent; there was even an ambitious newcomer to the established favourites calling itself the Antiques and Genuine Fake Stall with the engaging sub-title 'As not shown on T.V. Why worry about Arthur Negus? We've got it all here!'

One of Hooky's firmest convictions in life was that if you went to a swimming party there was no sense in being a spectator; the only sensible thing to do was to jump in and swim. He therefore had every intention of working his way slowly round the fête and sampling pretty well everything. With a view to practising his throwing for the match next day he decided to make a start at the coconut shy. A red-faced villager, oozing bogus geniality, welcomed his custom. 'Try your luck, sir. Three balls for 5p; eight balls for 10p. Take away any nuts you knock out. Have a go.'

Hooky duly paid over a ten-pence piece and began to select eight wooden balls from a basket full of them close to the thrower's mark. The balls had obviously done duty before at many a previous fête and a number of them were chipped and imperfect. Hooky was in the process of rejecting the worst specimens and gradually accumulating his chosen eight when a voice at his side assured him, 'It won't make no difference, mister.'

Hooky suspended his process of selection to see who was giving him advice. It turned out to be a small boy (aged eight or nine, he supposed) with an abnormally large head and a hideous squint only partially corrected by powerful glasses. Through those steel-rimmed glasses two preternaturally sophisticated eyes viewed Hooky sardonically. The tadpole-like head now shook in confirmation of the information already given. 'It won't make no difference, mister, which balls you chuck. You won't knock no nuts down.'

Hooky was rather proud of his throwing ability. 'Want to bet on it?' he enquired amiably.

'Anything you like,' the Horrible Child assured him with suspicious alacrity.

'What makes you so sure I can't knock a nut out?'

'Uncle Albert glues 'em in too firm' was the disconcerting reply.

Despite this useful inside information Hooky completed his selection of the heaviest eight balls he could find and did his best, concentrating his attack on one particular coconut which stood slightly in front of the rest. Four balls were misses, but with the remaining four he scored direct hits; he was throwing with all his might and in each case the ball ricocheted off the nut and flew into the stop-netting at the back of the stall at high speed. The coconut, however, remained as unmoved as the Rock of Gibraltar. The Horrible Child nodded his tadpole head in gloating satisfaction. 'Told you so, mister,' he said.

Hooky marched on to the Roll-'em-in, which had the advantage, from his point of view, of being run by a girl who, had there been a competition for Buxom Village Wench of the year, would undoubtedly have come out on top. The Buxom One smiled when she saw Hooky approaching, thus following the fashion of most women throughout his life.

'Roll your own 5p pieces down,' she intoned. 'Clear the lines and pick up a fortune. You can't lose.'

This optimistic prediction proved entirely false as far as Hooky was concerned; fascinated by what can only be described as the Ultra-Buxomness of the Wench he stayed for some time at her stall hopefully rolling one five-pence piece after another down the little inclined chute. Each time the coin, after a certain amount of wobbling hesitation which only flattered to deceive, finally settled not in the middle of a numbered square which would have won him a reward but fouling one of the dividing-lines which won him nothing.

At length his supply of five-pence pieces was practically exhausted. 'Bad luck,' said the Buxom One, smiling broadly. 'Still, unlucky at gambling lucky at love, so why worry?'

'Shall I show you how?' said a voice at Hooky's elbow. He turned to see the Horrible Child there.

'If you lend me a 5p bit I'll see what I can do,' the H.C. told him.

Mesmerised, Hooky produced a coin and handed it over in silence.

'The trick is to start them about halfway up, like this,' the expert said, placing the first coin midway up the inclined chute and releasing it with a curious stroking movement of a chubby forefinger. It rolled on to the marked board, wheeled to the left, lost impetus and sank to rest clear of all lines right in the centre of a square marked 6. The Buxom One handed six five-pence pieces to the Horrible Child.

'And my own back again,' the H.C. said. 'I wasn't born yesterday.'

'Pity you were born at all,' the Buxom One said with feeling, a sentiment with which Hooky felt some sympathy.

'That's how it's done,' the Horrible Child told Hooky, squinting at him through powerful glasses.

'I'm sure it is,' Hooky agreed. 'Meanwhile what about my 5p?'

'Ah, I was forgetting that.'

'I wasn't. What I lend I like paid back. Fork out, chummy.'

It did not surprise Hooky in the least that when he came to a halt in front of the next sideshow – the Shooting Gallery – the Horrible Child was there by his side.

'I suppose you know all about this, too?' Hooky said as unpleasantly as he knew how.

The large head nodded in confident affirmation. 'Yes, I do. That old rifle pulls to the left. You want to aim at the right-hand edge of the target to get a bull.'

Reflecting that omniscience was one of the most irritating things in the world, but also one most foolish to despise, Hooky took careful aim at the right-hand edge of the small square target and pressed the trigger. The youth looking after the stall was effusively complimentary. 'Bang in the middle. A perfect bull. Lovely shot. Have a goldfish.'

A bull apparently entitled the scorer to a minute goldfish swimming unhappily in a tiny, imprisoning, glass bowl not much larger than the poor unfortunate fish itself. Hooky declined his prize. 'Do you want it?' he asked the Horrible Child.

The H.C. shook his head. 'I've much better ones at home,' he said. 'My lot would eat that thing. Is it right you're playing in the cricket match tomorrow, mister?'

'That's the idea.'

'Play for the Three Foresters or something, don't you?'

'*Free* Foresters, chummy.'

'Free? Does that mean you're an amachewer? I call that barmy. I wouldn't do anything unless I was paid for it, not a thing.'

'And the way things are going,' Hooky said, 'you are likely to grow up to be a worthy addition to the sporting scene.'

Finally Hooky found himself outside the Fortune Teller's tent – 'Zolanda, Palmist and Clairvoyante, Characters and Fortunes Told 50p,' the notice said.

'Her name isn't really Zolanda,' the inevitable voice said at his side. 'She's Mrs Evans; she's my mum's sister. Ask her if you're going to make a hundred tomorrow, mister.'

As this was precisely the question which Hooky had contemplated asking the wind was rather taken out of his sails, but he dismissed thoughts both of consultation with Zolanda and of the Horrible Child when, suddenly, he saw Charlie Pentallan approaching across the lawn. At least one firm principle had served Hooky well in his life – 'Never apologise, never explain, never bear a grudge' – and, although his last meeting with Charlie had ended in high words and a certain amount of temper and, indeed, in his own dismissal, he no longer harboured any trace of resentment about it. He was delighted to see that Charlie evidently felt the same way.

'You've come to play in the cricket match, haven't you, Hooky?' he cried. 'I heard about it from Skipton.'

'I had promised Tom Pacey I'd turn out and I couldn't let him down.'

'No, of course not. I don't believe you would ever let anybody down.'

'All testimonials thankfully received,' Hooky said; it struck him that his ex-employer was in a very ebullient mood. 'How are things down here?' he asked.

'Oh, much the same, you know; but actually no, it's silly to say that. Why do we say silly things, Hooky?'

'Because on the whole we are a silly lot of fools,' Hooky informed him. 'What's different, then?'

Lord Pentallan nodded towards Zolanda's tent. 'Are you going to have your fortune told?' he asked.

'I did think about it; but on the whole I think I'll save my 50p. By and large I reckon I know more about my fortune than Zolanda does. Are you having half a quid's worth?'

'Yes, I am. And I know what she's going to tell me; she's going to tell me that everything is going to be all right and that I'm going to be tremendously happy.'

'Well, it's worth 50p to know that any day.'

'I mustn't name any names at the moment, but I expect you know what I'm talking about, don't you, Hooky?'

'I can make a guess.' Hooky studied the young man in front of him, in some ways so much younger than his years. Hooky had liked him from their first meeting and still liked him. 'You're sure you aren't making a mistake?' he ventured to say.

'Absolutely sure. I'll be able to tell everybody about it in two or three days, I expect.'

'Well, good luck to you,' Hooky said. 'One way and another that's what most of us need in life, a pretty sizeable slice of good luck.'

In the Arms that evening business was brisk and Tom Pacey was in great form; his new opening batsman of whom he expected so much had arrived and the rest of the team had been contacted and secured; it was now permissible to look forward to a glorious victory on the morrow; meanwhile all the regulars, Henry Capper among them, were steadily doing damage to their livers and good to his till in about equal proportions.

Hooky and the man from the *Advertiser* gravitated together naturally and inevitably.

'Tom says he's expecting great things of you tomorrow,' Capper said.

'I shall be lucky if I'm not out first ball. Are you covering the match?'

'And the Fête. I've done my bit on the Fête already.'

'I didn't see you there this afternoon.'

'I wasn't there; but you wouldn't expect that to stop me writing a column and a half of more or less deathless prose about the jamboree, would you? I've been to so many village fêtes, Hefferman, that all I need is the programme and a local name or two and I don't have to go near the place. Once in a while something sensational happens and, of course, that makes the going tricky. But that's an occupational risk. Nothing like that today, I suppose? The Hall didn't catch fire? No streakers? The Vicar didn't run amok and rape the President of the W.I.?'

'Not whilst I was there. In fact the head W.I. dame looked pretty well unrapeable, I'd say. No, no alarms and excursions.'

'How's His Lordship?'

Hooky suffered a minor conflict of loyalties; he would like to give this amiable old soak the chance of getting a good 'exclusive'; on the other hand, although no longer employed by Charlie Pentallan, Hooky felt a certain diffidence about giving away personal information about him, especially when, after all, it could hardly, as yet, be classified as hard news.

He contented himself with answering, 'Chirpy.'

Henry Capper's trade was words and he was alerted by this unusual one.

'Chirpy? What does that mean exactly?' he queried.

Hooky's face contorted itself strangely.

'What the hell's up?' Capper enquired. 'You going to have a fit or something?'

'That was a nod and a beck and a wreathed smile all in one,' Hooky told him. 'Very difficult to do actually. And that's all you're going to get from me.'

'Not being a blind horse I'll make note of same,' Capper said. 'Something in the air, is there?'

'No comment. What about the other half?'

On Sunday morning the first thing everybody in the village did was to assess the weather prospects. In spite of a hectic Saturday night in the bar Tom Pacey was up betimes; stand-in his shirt sleeves in the yard of the Arms he surveyed the sky, smelt the wind and made his forecast.

'She'll behave herself today,' he thought. 'She'll be a good one. Baking hot, most likely, time the first ball is bowled.'

Tom had a busy day ahead of him. The Arms itself would be open as usual, but in addition there was the refreshment tent on the cricket ground to prepare; lunch to think about for thirty people (Mrs Pacey was already in the kitchen) and, supreme dominating matter of all, the match itself.

The match was due to start at twelve and lunch for players and officials was scheduled for one-thirty, so Tom was well aware that there was not going to be a minute to spare getting things ready.

Up at the Hall Charlie Pentallan was also up earlier than usual on a Sunday morning. Saturday afternoon's fête had created a certain amount of disarray and untidiness in the grounds, and since he had been warned that the first coach-load of visitors would be arriving to view the gardens shortly after eleven o'clock he was anxious to get things straightened up as much as possible. He need not have worried; the Fête was an annual village affair; the village knew how to handle it, what was required and what everyone's responsibilities were in the matter.

Helpers turned up unbidden, and with Skipton and Mrs Skipton directing and assisting the work of restoration went along famously.

Charlie was looking forward to the events of the day. The cricket match itself meant very little to him, but he was due to meet Dolly on the ground at half-past two and to spend the afternoon with her watching the game. In the curiously withdrawn and sheltered life which he had so far led, Charlie had never before been so much influenced by a woman as he had come to be lately. He imagined himself to be in love, and imagining oneself in love was an intoxicating and exciting experience; it was a time for being happy; and Charlie was sure, most of the time anyway, that he was happy. Every now and again he was worried for a moment because Dolly had not given him the answer he wanted straight away; but any worries on this score were easily dismissed when he reflected that all his life he had made mistakes by being too impetuous and that her request to have time to think things over for a while was absolutely reasonable and sensible. Of course, there was the 'Mrs Acton' business; she hadn't told the truth about that to start with; but, then, as Hooky Hefferman had once said (and later Charlie himself had echoed), we are all of us liars at some time or other and about some things. Charlie had been glad to see Hooky at the Fête on the previous afternoon; he hoped to have a triumphant piece of news to convey to him before the day was out.

Some time after eleven o'clock Charlie was crossing the hall when a stranger came in through the wide-open front door. Imagining that the man was part of the coachload of visitors due to arrive during the morning Charlie said, 'I'm afraid the house itself isn't on view; it's the gardens you've come to see.'

The stranger disregarded this piece of information. 'Are you Lord Pentallan?' he asked.

'I am, yes.'

'You're the chap whose father died in that club a little time back?'

'It was my uncle actually. May I ask who you are and what you want, please?'

'I think you know a woman calling herself Mrs Acton, Dolly Acton!'

The introduction of Dolly's name startled Charlie; suddenly there was something hostile and menacing about the whole situation and he didn't like it.

'What have you got to do with Mrs Acton?' he asked.

The man looked round the hall. 'Do you want to talk out

here?' he asked. 'Or isn't there somewhere a bit more private we can go?' He laughed disagreeably. 'Mind you, *I* don't mind; I know all the unpleasant things. You're going to get the shocks.'

Charlie turned and led the way into a small room usually called 'the office' which he used as a study. The man followed him in and Charlie shut the door and asked, 'What shocks? What are you talking about?'

'Well, for one thing she isn't Mrs Acton at all and never has been.'

'I know that. Dolly told me that.'

'Did she, indeed? I bet there was a hell of a lot else she told you too.'

Charlie was beginning to get angry.

'Who are you?' he demanded. 'And what on earth are you doing here?'

'Keep your hair on, Pentallan,' the stranger advised him. 'In one of her reports on the situation Dolly told me you had a habit of flying off the handle; there's not much point in doing that; it won't get you anywhere.'

'In one of her reports on the situation? What do you mean by that?'

Daley laughed unkindly. 'You're a bit of a mug, aren't you?' he said. 'You want to know who I am. Well, I'll tell you. I'm the man your dear little Dolly has been living with for the past five or six years; and very nice too; some of it; when she's in the mood.'

Charlie Pentallan went white, and watching him Daley laughed again. When he had set out from London his intention had been to go first to Gorse Cottage and have a flaming row with Dolly herself, but in the train he had altered his plans; it was clear to him that the scheming bitch had decided to ditch him and go off on a ploy of her own and he came to the conclusion that he could probably do most harm to her plans by going straight to the man she was making a fool of.

'Oh, yes,' he went on, 'you'll find her all right in that way, when she wants to be; but don't believe a word she says; I strongly advise you not to do that. I suppose she has told you about how she came to take this Gorse Cottage place, has she?'

Dimly aware at the back of his mind that he ought to be throwing this horrible stranger out on his ear, and yet at the same time conscious of a dreadful feeling that everything was collapsing round him, Charlie, half-hypnotised, asked in a flat, toneless voice, 'What do you mean, how she came to take it? She leased it from Colonel Fellows.'

'And I suppose she told you that Colonel Fellows was an old friend of hers.'

'Yes, she did.'

'And you believed her? Well, why shouldn't you? She's good at the game. She's made mugs out of plenty of men before you. Now it's your turn. Dolly had never heard of Colonel Fellows till she happened to see his advert in the personal column of *The Times*. Charming cottage, etc., etc., to let near Farnbridge. Near Farnbridge. That was the point. That's what she spotted.'

'Farnbridge?'

'Let's start at the beginning, shall we? Take it slowly. Words of one syllable. The day your uncle passed out in his West End club Dolly was sitting in the flat with me, where we live together, and she saw the para about it in the *Evening Standard*. It didn't mean a thing to her except that your name was mentioned as being the heir and coming in for the money and the estate and so on. Charlie Fenton. That reminded her that twelve years ago at a pub in Maidenhead you and she had got mixed up in the same party somehow. She said that in those days you were a young fool without any money and now when you were a bit older you might still be a fool but you had come in for a lot of it.'

Charlie listened in silence, staring at the objectionable stranger and trying to fight off the dreadful conviction that what he was hearing had the ring of truth about it.

'In that account in the *Standard*,' Daley went on, 'it spoke about the Pentallan estate near Farnbridge, and a couple of days later "Farnbridge" was the word which caught Dolly's eye in *The Times* advert. That's the way things happen in life. People may not believe it, but it is a fact that half the successful swindles that get pulled off start with some sort of lucky chance or coincidence like that.'

'Swindles?'

Daley laughed in derision. 'For God's sake, don't sound so surprised,' he said. 'You're acting like a kid who still believes in Father Christmas. Yes, swindles. Money; your money. What else do you think she came down here for? She intends to get twenty thousand pounds out of you, and from the look of you I should think she very probably will.'

'Twenty thousand pounds.' Poor Charlie repeated the words in a dazed way; he was so horrified by what was being said that he made no protest against the brutal manner of the saying.

'That's the nice little sum she intends to lift off you, Pentallan; and if you take my tip you'll cough it up straight away and send her packing. Save you a lot of trouble in the long run.'

'But what about Jimmy Loader?'

Daley shook his head. 'I haven't the faintest idea what you're talking about, but she's sure to have somebody working the scheme with her; he'll get his cut, Dolly will take hers and, like I said a moment ago, you're the mug. She'll be laughing her head off over you when all this is over.'

Charlie Pentallan lowered himself slowly into a chair and sat staring at his disastrous visitor. He was deathly white.

Daley looked at him for a few seconds and then laughed again. 'Well, I thought I'd just let you know,' he said, 'in case you want to do anything about it.' With that he went out of the room and Lord Pentallan was left sitting there, shaking. Presently he got up and almost as though in a trance walked out of the study across the hall and down the stone-flagged passage towards the gun-room.

* * *

A large, luxuriously appointed coach drew up in the forecourt outside the Pentallan Arms and from the doorway Tom Pacey viewed it with extreme satisfaction.

The other side. The Thirty-second. The regiment. The old mob. Different men from his day, yet essentially the same. Tall, lusty, fit, aggressively masculine. With their wives, sweethearts, concubines, girl friends, man pals. The whole boiling of them thirsty and raring to go.

'Lemonade for you lot, then, is it?' Tom greeted them, 'Beer's off.'

'It better hadn't be,' they assured him, invading the place in a wave of laughing, talking, joking humanity, shouting out greetings, orders for drinks, messages from old comrades of former days and dire threats about what was going to befall the local side. In his shirt sleeves, working like a demon behind the bar, Tom Pacey was happy; the thought didn't actually occur to him, but it might well have done, that Paradise, if it existed, would be something like this.

Halfway through the preliminary drinking session a small fly appeared in the ointment.

'Let's have the score-book, then, Tom, will you?' the captain of the village side said.

Tom Pacey looked up sharply in the act of drawing a pint of bitter.

'I haven't got it,' he said. 'You have.'

'Not me, Tom; no.'

'You must have, Bill.'

Bill shook his head. 'Not set eyes on it since last time,' he averred.

The score-book was a sacred object; it stretched back to the first game between the village and the Thirty-second and by now was an invaluable repository of old names, facts and figures. Its loss would not only be an inconvenience, it would be a disaster; and for a moment Tom was in consternation.

'Wait a moment, though,' Bill said. 'Didn't you let the Colonel have it after the last meeting?'

Tom nodded in vast relief. 'Quite right. I did. It'd be on that desk of his with all his cricketing books, I shouldn't wonder.'

Bill looked round. 'Anybody know the lady that's taken Gorse Cottage, Mrs What's-her-name?'

'Acton,' Hooky Hefferman said. 'Yes, I do. I'll go and ask her for the score-book if you like.'

'That's good of you, Mr Hefferman,' Tom said. 'You know what it will look like, the usual sort of thing, a big more or less square thing with a green cover.'

Dolly was surprised when Hooky poked his head in through the doorway of Gorse Cottage, open to the summer morning, and asked if anyone was about.

'I thought Charlie had got rid of you,' she said, but the remark had no real venom in it. Even if he had disappointed her in the past Hooky was a cheerful chunk of masculinity for a woman to see around.

'Bad pennies have got nothing on me,' Hooky assured her. 'I've come to play in Tom Pacey's match.'

'I shall be there to watch you,' she told him. 'I'm meeting Charlie on the cricket ground at half-past two. Will you be batting, or whatever it is, then?'

'How the devil do I know?' Hooky said amiably. 'It all depends how the game goes. And it won't even start unless we can find the score-book. That's what I've come for.'

'The score-book?' Dolly looked blank and irritatingly amused at the childish idiocies of men.

Hooky was already glancing round the room.

'From what Tom said it's probably on that desk in the corner. Can I have a look?'

'Help yourself.'

On the wall above the Colonel's desk was a shelf which carried nothing but cricketing volumes, and lying on top of them was the large, thin, green-covered book that Hooky had been sent to get. His hand was actually outstretched towards it when he heard a slight noise behind him. There wasn't time to analyse why the sound carried danger signals to him (E.S.P. perhaps?); but it did, and he turned round quickly to face the room. To his astonishment Charlie Pentallan was in the doorway and he was carrying a gun.

For a long moment the three figures were motionless, as though the scene were a 'still' cut from a film: the broad-shouldered, powerful man standing by the shelf of cricketing books; the woman, one hand halfway up to her throat, with fear dawning in her eyes; the man in the doorway, his face white and strained and a gun in his hand. The atmosphere of the room was suddenly filled with tension and with the apprehension of tragedy.

What the hell goes on here? Hooky wondered, studying Charlie Pentallan's face for some sort of clue. The man with the gun looked at him and asked, 'And how long have *you* been here?'

The woman took half a step forward and said, 'Charlie—'

'Don't Charlie me,' he said bitterly. 'I've been finding out a few things. What about the man you've been living with for the past five years? What about this cottage and Colonel Fellows? What about the twenty thousand pounds you have been scheming to get out of me? Not that I care about the money.' (Tears began to run down his white cheeks. The second time I've seen him cry, Hooky thought.) 'It isn't the money. I care about *you*. I thought – oh, God, never mind what I thought.'

Hooky, watching, a fascinated spectator, thought: *That boy's off his rocker. What the hell is he toting that gun for?* And then he noticed the beginning of a movement.

The instantaneous speed of human thought gave Hooky just time enough to reflect that very probably Charlie Pentallan hadn't much idea how to use a gun and would probably make a mess of it; but he wasn't taking any chances; as he hurled himself across the room the gun exploded and the woman started to scream.

Thirty seconds later, but it seemed a great deal longer to the three people concerned, Hooky had the gun in his hand and was viewing in a detached way the blood coming from the fleshy part of his right arm; Dolly had sunk into a chair, and Charlie Pentallan was leaning against the wall by the side of the doorway almost in a state of collapse and now blubbering freely.

Hooky broke the silence.

'I told you before that you were a bloody young fool,' he said, 'but I didn't know you were such a bloody fool as that.'

Charlie covered his face with his hands and said, 'Oh God.'

'You mustn't go round playing with guns, Charlie boy,' Hooky advised him. 'Not your line at all. If you go on like that you'll hurt somebody some day.'

'*Are* you hurt?' the woman asked, and Hooky was relieved by the lack of hysteria in her voice. That one's all right, he thought; she'll keep her head. And he admired her for it.

He had already done some investigation, enough to know that he was lucky. The bullet had merely grazed his arm and what wound there was, although messy at the moment, was not of any real consequence.

'Nothing to worry about,' he told Dolly. 'Your boy friend isn't much of a shot. If I were you I'd get him in a corner and give him a good talking to. I'll get this lot tidied up down at the pub.'

'I could do it for you here.'

'Not to worry. Mrs Pacey will slap a bandage on me and Tom Pacey will pour a lot of Pimms into me and in half an hour I shall be as right as rain. But I'll take the gun with me. Where's that score-book I came for?'

Hooky put the gun away safely in the boot of his Jag which was standing in the forecourt of the Arms; and did so only just in time. Police Constable Evans, the Pentallan bobby, came in sight as the lid of the boot was closing.

'You had an accident, sir?' the good constable enquired, his professional interest alerted by the sight of blood on Hooky's arm.

Hooky had a respect for the Law, but long experience had

taught him the wisdom of never tangling with it if that could possibly be avoided.

'Bit of a one,' he answered. 'Nothing to worry about.'

'How did that come about, then?'

Hooky was good at this kind of game. 'Usual sort of idiocy,' he explained airily. 'You know, not looking in the right place at the right time. Then all of a sudden wham, bang and you've had it.'

P.C. Evans considered this and on the whole didn't get much out of it; finally all he said was, 'You'll want to stop that bleeding, sir.'

'I'll get Mrs Pacey to put a bandage on it.'

'Can't do better than Mrs Tom,' the policeman answered him. 'She'll fix you up all right. She's the Red Cross queen around here.'

Hooky nodded; and, not wishing to attract attention in the bar, went into the Arms by the back way.

P.C. Evans looked after him reflectively, troubled by a vague instinctive suspicion that he was missing something.

Comforting himself with the thought that he could ask Hooky some further questions later on in the day, Evans continued on his way to Pentallan Hall where he was to be on duty for the first part of the afternoon. It was a regular assignment on Fête Day, and since the visitors who came to look at the gardens were nearly all coachloads from various W.I.s there was hardly ever anything to be done and somehow an opportunity usually cropped up of a visit to the back door of the Hall and a glass of beer with Mr Skipton. Things were once again working out along this normal and uneventful programme when to his surprise P.C. Evans was accosted by a well-dressed, sensible-looking lady with something of a masculine ring in her voice.

'Constable—'

Evans turned round quickly.

'Anything I can do for you, lady?' he enquired.

'I've come here with a W.I. party from Dalesford – that's my village – and I've just recognised somebody.'

'Recognised somebody, madam?'

'You see that man, standing there on the lawn, by the edge of the big herbaceous border....'

Evans saw a man standing there; someone he didn't know; a stranger to Farnbridge.

'He's a swindler.'

'A swindler?'

'A – what do you call them? – a *confidence* man, isn't it?'

'A confidence man?'

'He came to my house, oh, weeks and weeks ago now, and tried to swindle me out of five hundred pounds. In fact, I actually gave him a cheque; but, thank goodness, my brother got it stopped in time at the bank.'

'Are you sure about this, madam?'

'Absolutely certain. His name is Major Beresford. Or, at any rate that was what he was calling himself then. He completely took me in at the time and then afterwards my bank manager made enquiries and the whole thing turned out to be a hoax. I'll come with you and confront him with it if you like.'

'Perhaps you had better, madam.'

Bernard Daley was standing looking at the flowers and shrubs in the long border not from any love or knowledge of gardening but simply because he was turning things over in his mind and debating what to do. He had intended to find his way to Gorse Cottage and have things out with Dolly, possibly beating her up in the process; but he was beginning to change his mind. He reckoned that his visit to Pentallan Hall had been entirely satisfactory. The young fool there had had his eyes opened all right and Dolly wouldn't get any further in that direction. Instead of having a row with Dolly he thought he would simply have no more to do with her. Cut her right out. Not give her another penny and close the door of the flat against her; after all, he had got Eva....

He was interrupted in these musings by a voice at his elbow.

'I'd like to have a word with you if I might, sir.'

Daley turned to see something which he didn't at all care for, a policeman's uniform.

'Major Beresford—'

Daley's eyes went quickly to the woman by the policeman's side. He knew her at once: Dalesford ... pruning roses in the front garden ... City Properties Development Association ... the whole thing nicely in the bag apparently, and then at the bank nothing and the smell of danger. There could be danger here, too, he thought.

'I'm afraid you are mistaking me for somebody else,' he said.

But when he had first caught sight of the woman who addressed him as 'Major Beresford' there had been, just for a second, a look of startled recognition in Bernard Daley's eyes; and P.C. Evans had seen it there.

We've got a fly one here, the policeman thought.

'Your name isn't Major Beresford, then, sir?' he asked.

'Certainly not.'

'Quite so, sir. The only thing is this lady thinks you might be this Major Beresford and she is making certain allegations against him; so if you wouldn't mind coming down to the station to establish your identity we can clear the whole matter up, can't we, sir?'

'It's completely unnecessary to go to the station,' Daley blustered.

P.C. Evans was used to blustering and in fact was rather relieved to see it; people who blustered usually had something to hide. 'I think it would be more satisfactory if you did, sir,' he said. 'This lady can come too. There's a police car in the drive so we can all go together.'

A great deal of drinking was done at the Pentallan Arms that evening. The Thirty-second were a thirsty lot and they performed manfully amongst the beer; the village, not to be outdone and with the sheen of victory upon them, matched them pint for pint. Hooky had been expertly attended to by

Mrs Pacey, but all her protestations that he mustn't think about trying to play cricket with an arm like that went unheeded. Which angered her and outraged her Red Cross instincts.

'Well, all I can say is that you're very stupid if you do,' she declared roundly.

'Men are stupid, Mrs Tom,' Hooky said in a placatory way. 'Hadn't you noticed?'

'God help the world,' the good woman said, 'with men in charge of it.'

In the event, Hooky went in not at number one but at number eleven, his bandaged and strapped-up arm hardly allowing him to hold a bat.

When he came in Tom Pacey's side needed two runs for a tie, three for victory. The bowler was a fearsome creature, a six-foot-three Corporal P.T. Instructor, who hurled the ball down at an alarming speed.

In any circumstances Hooky wouldn't have much fancied facing him; with virtually one effective hand he didn't fancy the situation at all. The first delivery came so devastatingly fast that Hooky saw very little of it. More in self-defence than anything else he stuck his bat out and the ball fled off the shoulder of it high over the uselessly outstretched arms of the slips and raced to the boundary. Four runs; victory for Tom Pacey's side by two. 'That's what comes of having a class bat in your side,' Tom explained to all and sundry during the long subsequent evening in the Arms.

Serving Hooky with his third Pimms. Tom Pacey said, 'I see your friend Lord Pentallan came to watch you play, Mr Hefferman; he was sitting there with that lady from Gorse Cottage, Mrs Acton.'

Hooky laughed.

'The world's full of idiots,' he said. 'But, you never know, it might be all right. They might make a go of it. Sorry there's a smear of blood on the score-book, Tom.'

Tom Pacey didn't mind about the blood on the score-book.

'That'll remind me of a great victory,' he said.

Hooky raised his glass and drank. 'Well, things might have been worse,' he agreed.